The Absinthe Fountain

and other stories

Denmark Laine

Spartan Press
Kansas City, MO
spartanpresskc.com

First Edition: 1 3 5 7 9 10 8 6 4 2
ISBN: 978-1-952411-60-1
LCCN: 2021935595

Author's photo: B.M.R.

Table of Contents

THE
ABSINTHE
FOUNTAIN

PART I

The Black Cats

BranderGaz

Sebastian Prentice

Black Cat Riot Paradise St!

The Wormwood Quarter was rocked last week by a devastating explosion at the Plumbum Foundry leaving three workers dead and others severely injured. The building was left in rubble and the ensuing blaze spread to consume a city mile. The anarchist group known as the "Black Cats" are presumed responsible for this heinous attack, the latest in a string of bombings in and around the Noxhold area. Reports from the E.K.C.I. confirm that Black Cat agents have perpetrated five other malicious acts of wanton vandalism within the last month to further their campaign of terror. Lord Magistrate Ellery Fathom, Inspector General of the Scarlet Guard, has dispatched troops to investigate. The architect of these crimes is widely considered to be the so called "Paradise Street Dynamiter."

A key instigator among the rabble rousers wanted in connection with murder, arson, burglary, high treason and inciting civil unrest, whose identity remains unknown. A riot broke out on Paradise Street in front of the old Foundry where

Rer
foll
imp

The
that
rela
the
beh
of a
exp
in l
its
beh
con
or v

It m
tota
thir
dec
mo

CHAPTER ONE
THE MANY DEATHS OF
PROFESSOR ASCALON BROWN

Learn Forever, Yield Never. That was the motto of the Bal Cypress Club; the prestigious literary society that met on the first of each month in the Library Tower of Brander. These words engraved in the beveled glass window above its tall doors greeted visitors upon arrival. The Library Tower was a gnarl of gray pewter capped by a green, glass dome. The highest point in Brander, visible from anywhere, it rose like a spindly needle around which the dreary city turned. A young man in a black greatcoat bundled through the fog-shrouded streets toward the feeble glow of distant lampposts that flickered between low, pointed rooftops and black chimneys half-hidden in billowing clouds of soot. After a late start he'd set out from his garret room at 14-B Yarwick Square, near the dry docks in the Wormwood Quarter, the working class district. He'd lingered too long at Hob's Inn, a corner tavern, wallowing over his fourth or fifth glass of absinthe. Its gentle delirium quelled his nerves and steadied his hand as he sipped its verdant nectar alongside factory workers, madmen, cripples and other doomed souls, his fears dissolving like so many sugar cubes burned and melted in ice water, stirred to oblivion with a slotted spoon. The essence of the "green goddess", her bittersweet dream-grace distilled from deadly botanicals awaited him like a seductive mistress in an emerald glass. He spent most nights with his downcast gaze lost among flowery hallucinations in a cloudy puddle of chartreuse. This fertile spirit, bottled muse and moral decay, was banned elsewhere in the city. Absinthe's fickle visions were said to not only lead to the creation of paintings, poems and opera – vices in themselves– but also to blackouts, coughing fits, insomnia, stillbirths and murderous ravings. He crossed Mercantile Lane on muddy cobblestones. Along the crooked alleys known as the "Blood Bowl" for their suffocating stench of raw meat, pigs' heads hung on hooks at a butcher's stall, plucked geese dangled from ropes, sheep's bladders, cow intestines and various gut-scrapings stained many a wooden cutting board. Fishmongers laid out their mounds of salt cod, crab and oyster. Street peddlers flogged their wares such as pigeon pie and jellied eel, boiled turnips, pickled eggs and laudanum drops from vendor wagons and handcarts. The bustling marketplace also carried goods from the Anican Trading Company who unloaded exotic cargo of tea, silk, rum and opium from Ismere and Ilphane off steamships at Port Caliburn. He passed the iron fence along Cloth Row that separated the garment sweatshops from Dogyard Home For Boys. The young man dreaded that filth-ridden hovel. The reformatory run by a cruel, odious hag children called "Mrs. Mutt", where he'd grown up as a starving foundling on their doorstep forced to endure the brutality of the workhouses. Sent each day to the Noxhold factories, unwashed, slept on straw bunks, survived on cold porridge. They shaved his head, boiled his clothes and subjected him to grueling slave labor for the first twelve years of his life. Dogyard produced little more than dirty pickpockets that infested the already crowded narrow pavement along with the diseased, deformed, maimed and mad. He averted his eyes as he hurried on. Were it not for a former schoolmaster named Professor Ascalon Brown he would still be there. Prof. Brown, a kindly widower with no children of his own, adopted the boy at the age of thirteen and paid his way through academia. The old gentleman was a gregarious recluse who lived on the first two floors of an undistinguished, somewhat rickety but cheerfully furnished terraced house near Gaslight Park. Outside his window atop a marble pedestal stood a lichen-crusted statue of Queen Vivian scowling down on passersby. Her outstretched arm –home to nesting pigeons– pointed east toward Morningtide Canal. Every night in his cozy, upstairs study Prof. Brown read to the boy from his leather armchair beside the fireplace.

"What's your name, lad?" the professor asked that first night, lighting his pipe.

"I don't have one," came the reply. "But surely you must! Come now, what did your mother call you?"

"I never knew her, sir. They say she took a dose of pennyroyal so's not to have me."

""Well, what did the woman at the orphanage call you?"
"The other boys say I'm 'the loneliest.'"

The professor tapped his umbrella on the grate, studying the boy through green-tinted spectacles.

""Thelonious?"" he said finally. "That has a nice ring to it. You know what you must do, don't you? The only thing to do when one lays a curse at your feet. Pick it up and wear it proudly!"

The textbooks the professor gave him were still prized possessions: *Golden's Table of Numeric Equations*, *An Introductory Primer To Common Law* and *DeBaliviere & Wexler's Essays On High Finance.* Once the senior lecturer on ancient linguistics at Everleague Academy and secretary for the Bal Cypress Club, Prof. Brown taught him that books were mankind's most invaluable resource and that the solution to the world's most insurmountable problems could always be found between the right pages. He set aside this memory as his shakes returned. He clenched his fist and tried to ignore the phantom flavor of anise and fennel haunting his mouth. The young man passed Hanging Sword Pawnbroker at the corner of Leviathan & Hemlock. In his pickpocket days he used to sell the odd snuff box or pocket watch for a few coins to buy hot buttered rolls when the orphanage gruel left his belly empty. From the top of the hill he could smell the sea air wafting across Morningtide Canal. Handing a copper piece to a soldier with the Scarlet Guard he crossed Tollgate Bridge into the Quicksilver Quarter and its wealthy Ivormain neighborhood. Soldiers –"redbreasts" as they were commonly called for the color of their uniforms– were only stationed to protect the upperclass. Dollhouse mansions of the idle rich with their straight, marble columns, horse-drawn carriages and lily pad gardens behind mossy walls were a welcome contrast to the grime and drudgery of the Wormwood Quarter. Fashionable men and women in satin pastels swanned leisurely outside Devine Brothers Emporium carrying bundles of paper-wrapped parcels. The women with their skirts of frothy lace held delicate squares of fragrant silk to their noses or a parasol against the whispering rain while the men in their dapper frock coats, embroidered vests and gold-topped canes stepped over puddles. He passed Allgood & Daw's Apothecary, a specialty shop for spices and herbs which he remembered fondly from visiting after school for its jars of confectionaries: marzipan, clove drops, rum balls, barley-sugar twists and violet pastilles. Next door, Merryweather Haberdashery displayed the city's most celebrated gentlemen's apparel from its shop window. When he was adopted, Prof. Brown brought him there to have his school uniform tailored. He was one of the few boys fortunate enough to attend Everleague Academy. Only sons from Brander's most distinguished families were permitted to attend the elite educational institution where they were trained in mathematics, science and engineering. Sadly, his foster father disappeared after his eighteenth birthday. During his final year boarding at the Academy he received a letter notifying him that Prof. Brown hadn't been to work at the Library Tower for several days, asking after his health and whereabouts. The following week an article in *The Brander Gazette* ran Prof. Brown's obituary claiming he'd died on a journalistic assignment covering the Scarlet Guard's ongoing battle with foreign raiders along the Rivers Ismere and Ilphane. The young man never remembered Prof. Brown mentioning such a dangerous errand. Stranger still, a month later the last letter he'd written to Prof. Brown returned in the post, its wax seal still unopened, with an explanation that Prof. Brown couldn't be reached because he was overseas. The uncertainty surrounding his mentor's fate continued to weigh heavily. Further on stood the plain, windowless walls of Evenhall, the gray, craggy ministry building where the Evening King's Cabinet of the Interior, or "Shadow Cabinet" as it was sometimes called, held council. E.K.C.I. ministers were appointed aides and advisors to the crown who oversaw the nation's government. An ugly slab of modern architecture, imposing but utterly without ornament, it was a cold, rectangular block that interrupted the skyline like the city's unmarked gravestone. More eye-catching was the nearby Watchmaker Cathedral. A shining lattice of chrome cylinders built like a fifty-foot pipe organ, the Cathedral had as much warmth as the heavy cables, magnetic coils and rubber-cased turbines below which powered their photonic globes; artificial torches in glass orbs filled with spiral, wire filaments. Electricity was a fairly recent discovery only utilized within the last twenty years or so by an Everleague graduate, one Dr. Benjamin Ark. It was considered the height of modernity to replace gaslights in civic buildings with this latest invention, his patented "arklights." The Cathedral's highest turret was crowned with an immense striking clock built by Bal Cypress himself. It charted the astronomical procession of the moon on polished silver disks as a metallic octopus chimed loudly in the center, its eight legs dividing the hours. Watchmakers, as Cathedral members were called, in their immaculate white coats, strode in somber procession through that maze of laboratories, its cold, sterile depths presided over by Lady-Prior Adelaide Rossum, a minister in the E.K.C.I. Watchmaker Cathedral served as spiritual counterpart to Everleague Academy, applying the tenants of its curriculum away from experimental research to matters of moral enlightenment. "If one's endeavors could be attuned to the perpetual motion of the Clockwork," taught Mother Rossum, "then as in the material world, so too the inner world. As the stars align with the seasons, seedtime to harvest, day into night, even life unto death, these interlocking forces generate a cycle of balance and harmony that we may partner with if we act in accord with our purpose." The "Clockwork" referred to the state-sanctioned origin of the universe based on Bal Cypress' groundbreaking theory. All time and space, he wrote, are governed by "celestial gears" of order and reason. He saw the world as a great, self-regulating machine with humans working as necessary cogs. This ideology shaped the future of Anic's society. His Clockwork Theory ushered in a modern age of scientific industrialism. Everleague Academy was built to train students in the empirical study of nature while Watchmaker Cathedral indoctrinated them in obedience to their societal function for the betterment of their fellow man. In the center of the square he passed a high post on which was tacked an official criminal docket:

WANTED
High Treason
"Paradise Street Dynamiter"
Dangerous Arsonist & Enemy Conspirator
Guilty of murder,
destruction of public works,
inciting civil unrest.
Anyone with information as to the whereabouts of this fugitive must report to law enforcement immediately.
By order of
Lord-Magistrate Ellery Fathom
of the E.K.C.I. Inspector General of the Scarlet Guard

Thelonious shook his head as he passed. For years now he'd seen more and more reports of similar crimes; always the same senseless acts of vandalism. It seemed there was nothing anyone could do to stem the rising tide of dissent. Two blocks down at the end of Nightshade & Papyrus rose the Library Tower. Founded nearly a hundred years ago by royal historian Marlin Mendle, the Library contained thousands of books from every century of their nation's storied past within its treasured archives. The young man worked half his life to reach this moment. At the top of those stairs some of the most influential men in all of Anic met to discuss the ancient writings of famed philosopher, Bal Cypress, whose books included, *The Preludium: Anic's History & Legend*, and *Universal Clockwork: the Engine of Eternity*, to name a few. He'd read them as a student at the Academy. A metal pull-chain hung beside the door next to a plaque which read, "By Appointment Only. Ring Bell." Taking a deep breath, he nervously tugged the chain and a loud, hollow gong clanged from inside. After waiting almost ten minutes he was alarmed by the sudden crack of the heavy locks being turned which sounded like the splitting of a great tree. Finally the huge doors slowly edged open barely wide enough to reveal a decrepit man in a white, powdered wig.

"You're the new secretary?" asked the old man. He was dressed in the ceremonial gray robe of a royal librarian. A brass ring of keys hung from the sash tied about his waist.

"Yes. Yes, I am. How do you do?"

The old man ushered him inside and set to work locking back the tedious series of bolts and latches with his keys. They made their way up the stone steps until they reached the first landing when a mottled ball of tawny fur went yowling down the way they'd come. Startled, nearly knocked off his feet, the young man steadied himself against the wall.

"Don't mind him. That's Friendless, the cat. He's always getting trodden on." The old man's drooping shoulders and sagging, pockmarked cheeks hung low under his heavy-hooded eyes nearly hidden under bristly eyebrows that curled like horns. His eyes were beady and colorless while milkweed hairs sprouted unevenly from his chin. "I am Mr. Candlewick," croaked the old man. "Head Librarian. I've been asked on behalf of the Club to walk you through your duties."

"Pleased to meet you, sir," said the young man, extending a handshake, trying to still his fingers from twitching.

"Come, come," said Candlewick. "We may dispense with the pleasantries." He continued up the stairs, a light dusting of flour from his wig floated in the air behind him. "Thelonious Brown?"

"Yes sir." The old man ticked off each answer on a sheet of parchment with a quill pen. "And you're a recent graduate of Everleague Academy, are you not?"

"Correct."

"Your last position was at the Bank of Barnaby, Pontius & Gont?"

"Yes sir. Accounting clerk. Abacus Branch."

"Secretary for the Bal Cypress Club is quite an undertaking for one your age," cautioned Candlewick.

"Your responsibilities will encompass a great deal more than stacking numbers in tidy columns. The Library Tower contains each and every book in Anic." Thelonious chuckled to himself. He remembered Prof. Brown referred to the Library as a "room of answers" where all the wisdom in the world was locked away under one roof.

"I fail to see the humor in that, Mr. Brown."

"Nothing sir, it's just-"

"You'll find frivolity is an undesirable trait among librarians."

As they climbed upward in silence the shadowy steps growing dimmer around each curve, Thelonious felt the first misgivings about his qualifications for the job. After five minutes he felt a nagging ache of fatigue creep into his legs. Sweat beaded on his brow as he tried to wet his numb tongue.

"Certainly a long way," he said, attempting a brush with the convivial.

"Best get used to it," Candlewick suggested. "You'll be up and down these stairs at least twice a day, you know. One cultivates a tolerance after a while." As he spoke, they reached the top of the tower and the Library opened around them. Thelonious stood in awe. The maze of shelves–wall to wall, floor to ceiling, fifteen feet high, aisle after aisle in all four directions–sat empty. The Library contained nothing but gathering cobwebs. Thelonious could not conceal his shock. Then he noticed on the wall facing them were ten rows of books lined with no more than two hundred copies in total. *Is this…all?* he thought. He'd expected an endless multitude of books. Could the sum of Anic's knowledge really fill no more than a dusty corner? The sky's iron gloom became a murky green filtered through the jade dome above like the lid of a glass jewelry box. A painting of Bal Cypress over the stairs depicted the classical philosopher as a stern man with thick mutton chops the color of faded wheat that left his chin bare as a door knocker. He was pictured seated at his desk in a flowing gray librarian's robe and red cravat, writing on a scroll which fell to the floor, his free hand resting on a human skull which served as a paperweight.

"You were a ward of the late Prof. Ascalon Brown?" asked Candlewick, more to himself, reading aloud, scribbling away. Thelonious began to work up the courage to ask if there were perhaps more books elsewhere when Candlewick continued, "The professor's sudden passing was a grave inconvenience, I don't mind telling you. Unable to fill the vacancy on such short notice we were obliged to improvise. We found among his belongings a suicide note naming you as the next best candidate for this position."

"Suicide?" gasped Thelnious. "How?"

"Laudanum," came the reply. "A whole bottle was found empty by his bedside."

"I…I was under the impression Prof. Brown died some time ago."

Candlewick raised a shaggy eyebrow. "You two certainly couldn't have been better strangers." "He'd been away. Across the Puddle Sea. I assumed he perished in a shipwreck."

"Ascalon on an ocean voyage? Bah! You'd never get him out of his favorite armchair! Besides, do you think the Library has sufficient resources to send our secretaries gallivanting halfway round the world?"

Thelonious was dumbfounded, his thoughts suddenly clouded by doubt.

"I shouldn't mention any of this, if I were you," said Candlewick, "highborn Club members will not look kindly upon a commoner in their midst. Especially one whose merits are based solely on the favor of a dead man."

Stung by the insult, Thelonious bit his tongue and followed the librarian, coughing on his wig powder. In the center of the room was a polished oak table –its legs carved to resemble owl talons– set with a decorative silver teapot. Seated around the table were the members of the Bal Cypress Club. Thelonious could scarce believe he was in the same room as such famous persons: Lord Meredith Melrose III, an eccentric nobleman who owned a country estate in the Forty Corners, known for squandering his vast inheritance on parties and frivolous amusement. His interest in literary pursuits were that of a bored dilettante for whom prestige was his sole motive. Sir Pritchard Prentice, a wealthy newspaper publisher, owner of *The Brander Gazette* and foremost antiquarian book-collector. He'd spent a fortune over the years buying dozens of rare, illustrated manuscripts either at auction or from overseas imports, most of which he donated to the Library. It was the talk of the town when he flew across the Puddle Sea on an expedition with two airships, *The Valiance* and *The Libertalia*, bringing back exciting stories of sky pirates and the far away Isle of Lembria. But the most impressive guest was Dr. Osric Dropwort, Lord-Regent of Anic. He was a small man with jug ears and a long, beak nose giving him an impish appearance. Dropwort was Prime Minister of the E.K.C.I. making him the highest-ranking official next to the Evening King. Thelonious recognized other faces but couldn't name them. The men sat around drinking strong black tea; a fine Ilphanese blend of plum leaf, orange peel and bitter almond. They seemed to be in high spirits; their faces flushed, filled with laughter and noisy banter.

"Peace! What have we here?" shouted Lord Melrose.

"Gentlemen," Candlewick announced. "Allow me to introduce Mr. Brown, our new secretary." "Secretary? Guts and garters, they get younger every year! How old are you, boy?"

"Nineteen, sir."

"Why, he's scarce out of the nursery!" Melrose scoffed.

"He was hand-chosen by Prof. Brown to be his replacement," said Candlewick.

"Well," laughed Melrose. "Seeing as the old man is stiff as a board, this child certainly can't do any worse."

"Let him speak," Sir Prentice interrupted. "What have you read, boy?"

"I'm conversant with most of Cypress' early works," said Thelonious. "His *Preludium* and…"

"Everyone's read that!" Melrose groaned. "Can you tell me

where we might find this passage: 'one climbs a ladder to wisdom on rungs of folly'?"

"*The Tree of Robeion.*"

"Ha! Wrong! *Apples of Wisdom.*"

"I'm sorry sir, I don't believe that's correct."

"Of course it is, you impudent boy! *The Tree of Robeion* wasn't even written by Cypress! Do you presume to lecture me?"

"That's because the phrase in question wasn't written by Cypress," Thelonious explained. "It's attributed to his mentor, Palquin the Learned, chronicling the family line of Robeion. Cypress merely quotes him in *Apples of Wisdom*. So, originally, the passage belongs to Palquin."

The table fell to lively discussion as Melrose fumed silently, bested. "Well done, Mr. Brown!" cackled Dr. Dropwort, "One can always tell an Everleague man."

"Indeed," Prentice agreed. "A masterful knowledge of the period. Prof. Brown was right to recommend the lad."

Melrose stood to his feet. "Isn't it true that Ascalon Brown plucked you out of the gutter?" he bellowed.

"See here, your Lordship-" Prentice protested but Melrose cut him short.

"I heard that Brown –addlepated fool he was– took in some nameless, orphaned stray and dandied him up in noble garb to pass off as one of our own."

Melrose pointed a finger at Thelonious. "He may look the part of a scholar," he sneered. "But he's nothing more than a Dogyard pup in fancy dress! A lowly drudge, probably the bastard whelp of some Drollery girl!" Melrose pushed past them toward the door. "And I, for one, refuse to stand by while you tarnish this Club's reputation with his presence." The remaining members looked at each other, from one to another, uncertain how to react.

"Well, Mr. Brown, would you care for a cup of tea?" asked Dropwort. That provoked a few chuckles. Soon the whole assembly was talking again as Thelonious took a seat.

"Apologies for our colleague's behavior," said Dropwort. "Melrose has always been a petulant bore."

"An overdressed puff adder, more like," Prentice added.

"It's an honor to meet you, sir," said Thelonious.

"My dear fellow, are you feeling quite alright?" asked Dropwort, noticing his pale complexion.

"Fine, sir. Just nerves."

"When did you graduate?"

"Last year."

"Ah, then you must remember Headmaster Erasmus Manticore."

Thelonious recalled the aging chancellor of Everleague Academy. Campus whispers claimed the senile Headmaster was losing his wits. One term, Manticore locked himself in his study and wouldn't come out for days. As rumor had it, when he finally emerged he'd eaten the pages out of almost every book on his shelf. "Headmaster Billygoat" students called him after that.

"I knew your Prof. Brown," Dropwort added. "We were at the Academy together. Ascalon, Benjamin Ark, myself and others were particularly keen on any mechanical apparatus so we formed a workshop where we were allowed to experiment with our own inventions."

"I had no idea! Prof. Brown seemed more interested in books than tools."

"Ascalon was a great thinker as well as tinker. He had plans for a motorized hansom cab. Ingenious vehicle. Much like a carriage without a horse that achieved locomotion through an internal steam engine which powered its wheels."

"What ever became of it?"

"He wanted to find another fuel source other than coal. Never got the formula right. I, on the other hand, built what I called an 'eclipse reliquary'; a device to help astronomers view solar phenomenon without gazing directly at the sun through a telescope."

"How did it work?"

"A small mirror box with a convex lens would focus light into the darkened box onto a thin, silver-coated plate. Treated with bromine fumes and given the right exposure the silver plate, once removed, would capture a still image of the eclipse."

"Remarkable!"

"Oh, just a trifle, really."

"Gentlemen!" announced another man in a loud voice, whose name Thelonious thought was either Feverstone or Featherstone, "May we return to the topic at hand?"

"Get out your pen, Mr. Secretary," said Dropwort under his breath. "You'll be taking down the minutes of this meeting." Thelonious fumbled in his coat pockets.

"We were discussing the rising rate of sabotage," Feverstone continued. "Brander has become an insecure city teetering on the precipice of revolt. Over the past three months we've seen an alarming increase in industrial accidents."

"What do you expect from unskilled laborers?" another man chimed in. "Every week some daft bludger catches his arm in the mangle."

"A few injuries are to be expected, true," agreed Featherstone. "It's the cost of doing business. But what of the explosions in the Noxhold factories? This 'Paradise Street Dynamiter', as he's called? The workers rally around him despite the fact he's reduced most of them to shiftless beggars. The Plumbum Foundry was condemned last week. The damage to the building will take years to repair not to mention hundreds in taxpayer money. The unemployed litter our streets. Mark my words, gentlemen, it's those anarchists, those Black Cat radicals who are behind it."

Thelonious heard these reports in *The Brander Gazette*. He was familiar with Noxhold and Paradise Street; a more ironical name he couldn't imagine. Commonly known as "Death's Workbench", the Noxhold slum was a clamorous, overpopulated, urban furnace. He'd spent his boyhood toiling his fingers raw in the ash-covered assembly lines along Paradise Street. According to headlines, several factories reported incidents of machine-breaking due to tampering with their equipment: a rivet missing from a power loom in Cloth Row; a wrench thrown in the valves at Havenhurst Scrapworks jamming the conveyor belt spilling gallons of oil. Unconvinced that these disasters were mere coincidence the newspaper coined the name "Black Cats" for these saboteurs. However, the worst incident occurred the night the boiler in the Plumbum Foundry exploded destroying most of the building and setting fire to the roof. The Scarlet Guard investigated and ruled it was arson when they found evidence of dynamite packets in the rubble.

"One cannot reason with the illiterate masses," said Sir Prentice. "They act out of base instinct, motivated by anger and ignorance."

"True," agreed Feverstone. "But we've never seen them this organized. This united in a single cause. Arrest one and two take his place."

"It's this Dynamiter who's to blame," said someone else. "He's emboldened them. Become a champion to their plight. Every day he eludes capture is another day the strikes and riots grow worse. He ought to be locked away in Bellrath Prison and beheaded!"

"I think it goes deeper," said Featherstone. "Where did he learn to wreak such havoc? Blasting powder and munitions are not the talk and trade of your average shopkeeper. Where is he building these explosives? And, moreover, who is hiding them?" The men all shook their heads.

"The answer, gentlemen, lies in back rooms and cellars of every cheap public house, inn and stable where these Black Cats meet in secret to foment rebellion and plot to overthrow the government. Only last week three pantry boys were arrested at the Red Lion for stockpiling barrels of kerosene. The week before that, bricklayers at the Blue Boar were caught digging a tunnel which, had they completed it, would have reached under Evenhall itself! The Fiddle & Kettle, the Caretakers Arms and the Jack's Head were also raided in connection to seditious activity. My point is these extremists were all apprehended yet the Foundry was still demolished. Even as we speak, who knows how many similar treacheries are being perpetrated under our very noses? I say this Dynamiter is not one man, but many!"

The assembly went into an uproar, all arguing at once. Dr. Dropwort stood and motioned for silence. "Gentlemen, gentlemen, please! I assure you, on behalf of the Evening King, the matter is well in hand. My fellow Cabinet Minister, Ellery Fathom, the Lord-Magistrate and Inspector General of the Scarlet Guard has doubled our efforts in apprehending this vandal. A detachment of soldiers are searching the Wormwood Quarter from top to bottom, patrolling the streets on full alert for suspicious behavior. It is only a matter of time before this miscreant is found."

"And *if* you happen to capture another arsonist," said Feverstone. "What of the next one? And the next?"

Dropwort pursed his lips. "Then there will be a public execution of each and every suspect in our custody." That seemed to satisfy them for the moment and the conversation turned to lighter concerns. Dropwort sat down beside Thelonious, writing notes furiously.

"Did you get all that?" he asked.

"I think so."

"Then you'd better discard everything you've heard today."

"Sir?"

"It's inevitable, really. Politics and gossip. During this time of civil unrest it'd be irresponsible for us to encourage such rumors. And they are just that. Rumors, I mean. After all, an underground conspiracy masterminding a bloody revolution? The public is better served without us lending credence to such rank hysteria."

"I understand."

"Good man. By the by, I was sorry to hear of Ascalon. My deepest condolences. Horrible way to go. You, better than most, should understand why I hate these Black Cats."

"What do the Black Cats have to do with Prof. Brown's death?"

Dropwort looked surprised. "Why, he was waylaid in the street that night. On his way home when a group of young men beat him to the ground and robbed him."

Thelonious was speechless. "How…I mean, are you certain it was these anarchists? It could have been any thief or cutpurse."

"A black handkerchief was found near his body," said Dropwort.

"That's their signal. The way Black Cats identify one another."

CHAPTER TWO
HOUSE OF ZOS

From Bal Cypress' *Preludium: Anic's History & Legend*

It is written that Anic was created by Urzion the EverFather *during what is known as the* Preludium, the Time Before. *His long beard of countless gray hairs outnumbered the many worlds he created by writing in the* Book of Life, *a vast stone tablet he engraved with his finger. Whatsoever he wrote came into being. After writing the land, trees, mountains, rivers, Urzion grew weary and created others like himself to assist in his work. They were the* auldenarchs*: nine emanations of himself, each charged with creating one of the nine mortal races. The Anican Continent was given to a race called the* denae, *now known as man. They were created by* Zos, *the ninth auldenarch who stood for imagination. Zos was clever and endowed his people with more gifts than the other nine. He made Man immortal; the strongest, fairest, most magical race. When Zos created the first man and woman, King* Parlan *and Queen* Ilendere, *he made for them a house and told them its rooms were filled with all his secret wonders. Then Urzion grew weak and fell asleep at his book. In sleep, his hand continued to write. He dreamed of the void outside existence and he drew into being an immense giant called* Anic, *so tall it could drink from rainclouds like goblets. The Giant Anic terrorized the land, eating whole towns for breakfast and washing them down with lakes. This went on until the* Feast of the Bread of Ages *when the auldenarchs met to discuss what was to be done about Anic. Zos insisted the Giant must be destroyed; it was created by accident so it had no place in Urzion's world and would only undo everything they'd made. Some argued that it was not their place to say what Urzion intended and had no right to destroy their brother. Besides Urzion had not yet awakened from his slumber. None could say if he was finished writing in the Book of Life or not. The nine debated whether they should continue their work or stop where Urzion left off so as not to alter their master's creation. Fed up, unable to reach a unanimous decision, Zos tried to kill Anic himself. He bashed the Giant's head against a rock that was later called* Mount Horn. *From Anic's blood sprang creatures called the* etherials, *living shards of his mad, uncontrollable lusts. Order was restored when Zos trapped both himself and Anic inside Mount Horn, sacrificing his own power to imprison the Giant. From hence forth, all lands west of the mountain where the Giant was entombed bore the name "Anic."*

Thus marked the close of the Preludium and the end of the auldenarchs' reign. After King Parlan and Queen Ilendere's three sons had grown up, Prince Varthain *said to his brothers, "Come, let us go out into the world and build houses of our own." Prince* Relkin, *the eldest, was quiet and bashful and didn't venture outdoors for fear of trouble. But Prince* Andrel, *the youngest, was bold and full of action. He talked Relkin into joining them. When the three brothers snuck out to visit the forest at night with an axe to chop down trees for building material, at the first stroke of Varthain's axe a man in a yellow robe appeared before them shouting, "What is the meaning of this, Sons of the House of Zos?" He told them he was a ruler of the etherial courts, the creatures sprung from the Giant Anic's blood. He promised the princes that if they brought him what he desired from inside the House of Zos he would give them the greatest gifts the etherials could offer. To Relkin, a sword named "Beautiful" which he said could cut through anything, even death. To Varthain, a woman made from waterlilies to be his bride. To Andrel, a book which wrote itself. But they soon learned that gifts from the etherials are seldom what they seem.*

CHAPTER THREE
DIARY OF THE ROWAN KNIGHT

After a week, Thelonious settled into his new duties. He felt at home among the long, quiet corridors; the dry scent of paper and mildew; the forrest of rolling ladders which soared above mahogany archways to railed walks that encircled the uppermost shelves like castle ramparts filled with more echoes than books. His initial disappointment in the scarcity of the Library's contents had been replaced by grief over the professor's untimely demise. He had expected it would take a lifetime to read every book housed within these walls and relished the notion of getting lost perusing the "room of answers." Instead he'd already grown frustrated with little to do. He'd read what philosophy, science and history there was and Club members only requested one or two titles a month, mostly light poetry or novels. Still, as the new secretary Thelonious was made to swear Mendle's Oath. A brass plaque bore the inscription: "In the Name of Anic's Guild of Royal Librarians, the Benevolent & Fraternal Order of Robeion, First Scribe of the Written Word, I Hereby Undertake Not To Remove, Mark Or Deface Any Volume, Document Or Object Herein, Neither To Smoke, Strike Any Flint Or Tinder Nor Otherwise Kindle Any Flame." An ancient rule, now a meaningless formality, as paraffin lamps or anything flammable were strictly prohibited he worked by arklight; the bare glass bulbs glowing their ominous, cold fluorescence. He'd made no new acquaintances with other librarians, much less seen anyone other than Mr. Candlewick and Friendless, the old tabby, as he went about his daily routine. A few hours sorting through heavy, leather-bound tomes locked with rusty, iron clasps; rolled atlases on scrolls of yellowed vellum; books with intricate gold leaf designs etched on their spine; books with tatty covers worn and faded with pages falling out; books with charming illustrations of grapevines, flying ships, hourglasses, sundials, stone flowers, crown wreaths, mechanical insects, conch shells and languages in colorful script that looked more like music than words, and Thelonious had memorized the entirety of the Library's limited catalog. "Have you collected the books for the Club's next meeting?" Candlewick demanded.

"Yes sir," said Thelonious. "I've reviewed the list and I'm afraid, for a group that calls themselves the Bal Cypress Club, I've found precious little reading by Bal Cypress. Listen to some of these titles: *The Utility of Class* by Fredrick Lenore? *A Sportsman's Guide To Pheasant-Hunting* by Lord Ogglesby? *Bountiful Bess: Confessions of A Drollery Girl* by our own Sir Pritchard Prentice? None of these books were written by Cypress! They're not even from his period. They're modern."

"One cannot be expected to read the same books every year," Candlewick sighed.

"But surely this is a lot of bosh! No offense, sir," said Thelonious. "But our collection is sorely lacking."

Candlewick's bushy brow furrowed. "Lacking? You look upon the repository of all human knowledge and call it lacking?"

"Where are the books I read about at the Academy?" Thelonious protested. "Don't you see how much we must be missing? There are none of Cypress' contemporaries. Rivandar of Darfin, for example. Or Humphrey Throckmorton. Or Palquin's *Waltz of the Bonfires*. Or…"

"Mr. Brown," interrupted Candlewick. "The Bal Cypress Club is composed of the most preeminent luminaries in all of Anic. Our task is not to bore our esteemed guests to sleep but to keep them entertained. Their generous donations have funded the Library Tower so we might preserve our literary heritage which otherwise would have faded into obscurity. You should applaud them, not criticize them. Most people in this city cannot even read."

"Respectfully, Mr. Candlewick," said Thelonious. "You forget I was once among those illiterate masses. Were it not for the kindness of Prof. Brown I'd still be among them. These Club members, men of privilege, sit on a meager pile of information and squander it with their neglect."

Candlewick shook his wig, the powder floating like a small cloud. "It is you who forget yourself, Mr. Brown! For that impudence you are dismissed!"

Thelonious stalked home in a fury. Though he resented being treated like a fool he didn't mind being let go from the Library as much as he thought he would. The reality of that place paled in comparison to its reputation. A waste of time. Time which could be spent at a bar rapt in the green embrace. He bought a copy of *The Brander Gazette* from a passing stall and glanced at the headline on the front page:

PEASANT UPRISING IN FORTY CORNERS! ANOTHER RAG JACK RESISTANCE?

Lord Meredith Melrose found murdered by pitchfork. One field-hand, Hector Fetch, deemed responsible. Fetch, whom commoners proclaim "Hedge King, Hector the Protector, People's Champion of the Cornerlands", uses the regrettable accident of his nephew's death, a beggar boy trampled by his Lordship's horses, as excuse to recruit a makeshift army of farmers, blacksmiths and swineherds. This treasonous militia, his so-called "Gunpowder Gentlemen", are fighting to expel the noble families from the the Forty Corners and take the countryside for themselves. The villages of Blackthorpe, Farfallow and Shadeborough have already fallen to mob rule. His Gunpowder Gentlemen looted and burned the manor houses of the Middle Lords, turned them out in the cold, stripped naked, some even stoned to death. The E.K.C.I. has deployed the Scarlet Guard to put down the rabble and return the besieged farmlands to their rightful owners.

This was worrisome news. Thelonious harbored no particular affection for Lord Melrose who'd been rude to him on his first day, but he didn't relish the image of his Lordship skewered on a pike. The Forty Corners were the fertile breadbasket of Anic. Without their seasonal crops the food supply for their entire population could plunge into jeopardy. On the other hand, he knew the cruelty of the ruling class all too well. These hungry sharecroppers were retaliating against harsh living conditions, years of mistreatment and frustration that their annual harvest went to feed the cities instead of their own children. Ten short years ago the Scarlet Guard put down a similar insurrection, the Rag Jack Resistance. Led by a former soldier, the Rag Jacks swept into Brander pillaging their way up Mercantile Lane toward Morningtide Canal until they reached an army blockade at Tollgate Bridge led by Lord Magistrate, Inspector General Ellery Fathom. The Rag Jacks charged, chanting "redbreasts fly, redbreasts die!" The carnage that ensued was swift but brutal. Not a single man on the Rag Jacks' side was left alive. The Scarlet Guard were under Fathom's strict orders to take no prisoners. The resistance leader, the eponymous "Ragged Jack" or "Jack Patches", was put on display atop a wooden platform in the market square for weeks after holding his severed head in his lap as a warning to turncoats. "Bow your head or part with it" was the gory message. Every Midwinter's Eve Brander marked the occasion by hanging headless dummies as decoration made of old clothes stuffed with newspaper. Some used a rotten pumpkin for a head to chop off in mock execution as they laughed at the silly toy soldier who thought he could turn the world upside down. Around midnight at Hob's Inn, too drunk to move but too restless to sleep, Thelonious found he still had his old copy of *The Preludium* by Bal Cypress in his leather satchel. He'd read it many times at the Academy but leafed through out of boredom. It went on to document the Etherian Wars and how humanity was rendered mortal because King Parlan, mad with ambition, attacked the etherials, offspring of the Giant Anic, wrongfully blaming them for the death of Zos. It told of how King Parlan's eldest son, Prince Relkin, a great warrior, renounced his crown to live as a commoner believing he could do more good for his people by traveling among them righting wrongs. Prince Varthain, his second son, was a coward and a traitor who usurped the throne by plotting his father's murder. And Prince Andrel, his youngest son, fathered Robeion who began the lineage of royal scribes and bookkeepers, a tradition which led all the way to Marlin Mendle and the foundation of the Library Tower. This was a peculiar period in literature. Although such things as auldenarchs and etherials had been relegated to childish nonsense in light of modern technology, their nation's history was so intertwined with these legends distinguishing the credible from the fanciful was often impossible to parcel out. Even King Parlan, the source of Anic's monarchy, was now viewed as more of a symbolic figure than a flesh-and-blood man. At the Academy, Bal Cypress' early work was part of the curriculum merely as contrast between their older tradition of poetic storytelling and Cypress' later scientific research on the Clockwork. Thelonious blinked, straining to peer through the dim tavern. He swore he saw something move. Had a black cat streaked across the bar? It happened so fast. His breathing grew shallow. The sight of two, luminous green eyes hovering, watchful, still stung his mind. He reassured himself it was probably Friendless on the prowl for mice. Then he remembered the Library's pet was dusty orange, not black. Then he remembered he wasn't in the Library at all. Thelonious rubbed his eyes, worried, again, if whispers that absinthe caused hallucinations even days after one's last drink were more than morbid prattle. What with all this talk of Black Cats in the papers and anarchists lurking around every turn it was no wonder the lonely shadows began to suggest feline shapes to his fatigued brain. Resting on the barstool next to him Thelonious found a small, black book with no writing on the cover. Curious, he opened to the first page, handwritten in pen and ink:

Dear Reader, whomever you may be, I trust this diary finds you sound in body if not of mind. Such is to be expected when one is educated by those Clockwork fanatics that run the Academy. Meddlesome fools! What asses rule the realm! You needn't sift through these terse quibbles for clues as to my whereabouts. I've taken special precautions to obscure my identity. A necessity these days. For the purpose of these notes I shall refer to myself as the "Rowan Knight." This is, in no small part, due to my ideas are denounced as subversive, even treasonous, under the Evening King's administration. No doubt you too have noticed an errant madness that's swept our halls of higher learning. That gullible acceptance of a theoretical "god-machine" which remains largely untested and unproven yet is set forth in classrooms as inescapable fact. This notion of the Clockwork has been handed down from the Shadow Cabinet as the basis for everything we're taught to believe about ourselves, society and the natural world. It is a blight on our intellectual development. It mars the very purpose of scientific inquiry. For when the answer to the mystery of life's origin is a foregone conclusion already agreed upon by our leaders to suit their agenda, how can we ever hope to move forward into new modes of discovery? In these entries I hope to expound upon two questions and the conspiracy engendered to keep them unanswered. Put simply: "Why are we forbidden to study any subject that contradicts the Clockwork?" and "Is there really an Evening King?"

Thelonious was intrigued. The anonymous author, this "Rowan Knight", went on to point out that history as recorded was notoriously unclear with dates and details in ancestry, plagued with assumption and inaccuracies. Going back to King Parlan and Queen Ilendere, if they were indeed the first man and woman created by Zos, gave birth to three sons, Relkin, Varthain and Andrel, then where did their son's wives come from? Palquin postulates in *The Tree of Robeion* that Queen Ilendere took another husband after King Parlan's death. However, as no other men existed except her three sons, Marlin Mendle's *Annals of the Kings of Anic, Vol. I* addresses this problem by suggesting that Varthain lay with his mother after conspiring against his father. Relkin never married and fathered no children.

So Andrel must have wed the daughter of his brother Varthain by their mother Ilendere to father Robeion. Robeion's descendants eventually led to the Mendle family who established the Library Tower in Brander around the same time the Evening King came to power.

Mendle, of course, has ample incentive to paint our history as his family portrait as it concludes quite neatly with him at the top. The obvious answer – so obvious in fact as to be scoffed out the door by Mendle and his narrow-minded League – is that our first king and queen had many other sons and daughters in addition to the three princes. Other sons and daughters whose lives went unrecorded.

That never occurred to him. Thelonious remembered his fellow students used to joke, "The Tree of Robeion? Not a family tree so much as a family forrest!" But, no. It couldn't be. It was far too simple. If that were the case and Parlan's royal vein flowed much further than taught at the Academy, why had no one suggested it before?

In the hundred years of his reign no one has ever laid eyes on the Evening King.

Thelonious considered that claim. As a boy he remembered the Evening King's carriage passing through the streets during one Midwinter's Eve Parade, but the carriage windows were covered by blue curtains so he could not see inside.

According to Palquin's Waltz of the Bonfires, *one hundred years ago Anic was embroiled in a bloody civil war. The last matriarch of King Parlan's line,* Queen Vivian the Morningtide, *at the age of eighty-one had grown fat and sickly from life at court. She'd suffered a miscarriage at a young age and never produced a child of her own. The dispute over her crown lay between her niece,* Ana of Malchire; *her second husband,* Lord Reginald Dravinious Dreyton-Harlyle*; her sister,* Lady Delphine, *and her uncle,* Sir Merrick Mendle, *who served as her chief man-at-arms. Each of the Morningtides contested their right to rule. Years of political coups, assassinations and dynastic struggle ensued. The kingdom was divided between the family, each province loyal to a different heir. Until a landmark battle in the Forty Corners brought an end to the chaos when the scriptorium known as the* Bookhouse At Three Marys *burned to the ground.*

Palquin built it as a sanctuary for writing of all kinds. Three Marys was a public forum where men of learning could live and study, copying manuscripts and teaching commoners how to read and write. At the time Three Marys held the largest book collection in Anic. Although miles from the field of combat Three Marys was destroyed by a catastrophic fire that left the surviving villagers devastated. Generations of irreplaceable work were turned to smoke in a single day. As Palquin later wrote, "After that battle we mourned not only the living slain but also the long dead who, in the destruction of their writings, were lost to us a second time." It was later discovered that Three Marys had been a strategic target. One faction during the battle hoped to find a historical record that would verify their master's claim to the throne while the opposing faction had destroyed it hoping the records, if any, would never be found. A young advisor in Queen Vivian's court, her cousin, Marlin Mendle, *stepped forward with a solution to the crisis. Marlin advised the queen to construct a tower in* Brander *where they could consolidate every book throughout the realm into one place; a library for the preservation of their history where it could be properly stored and kept safe. On her deathbed, Queen Vivian decreed a proclamation naming Marlin Mendle her royal historian and that every book in Anic was now the property of the Library Tower and must be brought to the capital. Palquin was happy to comply for in such barbarous times he believed it was imperative to protect mankind's knowledge for posterity. Palquin sent letters to every province urging their scribes and sages to aid in collecting every book they could find. Too old to make the two hundred mile journey to the capital himself, Palquin sent his apprentice, a thirteen-year-old page boy by the name of* Bal Cypress. *Marlin met Bal at court and was amazed by the child prodigy. Young Bal was the son of a master clockmaker from the foreign city of* Bael-Perazin *who proved to be a brilliant polymath. Once the Library Tower was established Marlin, along with the late queen's council, delved into their great archive of books to find a rightful heir to the throne. Three weeks later, after pouring over thousands of historical records, they announced what became known as* Midwinter's Eve*: they claimed they found the last, true scion of Parlan's blood. A young man from the Forty Corners, who, for reasons of security, they refused to name. This young man, they said, was escorted at night in secret to Evenhall and placed on the throne without fanfare. This was most unusual as a royal coronation was always a time of great celebration. Marlin and the council, the first unofficial* Shadow Cabinet, *said their new king would not hold a public audience for fear of assassination, but would make his commands known through them. Economic and military power was consolidated by dividing the spoils of the vanquished. Lady Delphine was imprisoned for treason and her* *farmlands, the Forty Corners, were absorbed into the County of Brander. To avoid a similar fate, Ana of Malchire surrendered her fleet of ships to Marlin which became the basis for the* Anican Trading Company. *Lord Dreyton-Harlyle perished during the war and what was left of his retinue of hunters and watchmen formed the* Scarlet Guard, *the Evening King's personal enforcers under Sir Merrick Mendle who agreed to resume his position as chief military strategist only because his son, Marlin, headed the new administration. A war-torn nation breathed a sigh of relief, grateful for a stable government at last and accepted the pretense of a secret king as the cost for peace. Commoners took to calling this unnamed monarch the* "Evening King" *because his reign began under cover of darkness. With Marlin's guidance, Bal Cypress became the most celebrated writer of his lifetime. He made his career with a controversial new subject that'd risen to prominence in the recently industrialized city; a theory that the physical universe was, in itself, a kind of natural automaton. He formulated this idea by watching his father repair clocks, music boxes and other mechanical devices in his workshop growing up. Marlin instituted this notion of* "Universal Clockwork" *as academic doctrine. It appealed to Marlin and the new political order of the day because it suggested that if the world was an indifferent machine running without an operator then the people most qualified to lead were not nobility with tedious pedigrees but anyone clever enough to tinker with its inner workings.*

According to the diary the Evening King either died long ago leaving his Cabinet Ministers to rule in his stead, or there never was an Evening King to begin with; it was all an elaborate ruse for the Cabinet to assume their position of vantage. The Library had confiscated all the books in the land so who was to say if this "boy from the Forty Corners" was really a legitimate heir or not? The only evidence lay in the hands of the librarians. And present Cabinet Ministers were, by and large, friends or relatives of the original council.

The Shadow Cabinet is not the right hand of the Evening King, the Evening King is a kid glove for the Cabinet's fist. Taking away our people's books also took away their ability to read and write and, by extension, their ability to think for themselves. An unwitting populace is easier to control. Ours is a great, industrial nation at the mercy of mass ignorance, unjust labor and political corruption. The Library Tower wasn't formed to preserve knowledge but to restrict it, making it accessible only to a small group of dominant men.

Thelonious looked up. This was a serious accusation. Where had this diary come from? Half the city would be furious if they found it. Who could have written it? His hand shook slightly as he pondered the likelihood if simply reading it was an act of treason? The author was obviously someone with unrestricted access to the Library. The amount of research was uncanny. There were more passages cited than any dissertation he'd ever written at the Academy. This diary was the single most in depth, independent study of his nation's past he'd ever read. Politics, culture, literature; it was staggering how it all connected beneath the surface. Who was this "Rowan Knight" and why did that sound so familiar? Thelonious recalled a nursery tale Prof. Brown used to tell him recorded in Cypress' *Preludium*. He turned to the chapter:

Prince Relkin once came upon a meadow where every man, woman and child had fallen into a deep sleep. In their sleep they cried out, babbling without word or reason, making awful noises more akin to the grunts of hogs. Try as he might, Relkin was unable to wake them. After searching among the sleepers he found a knight in armor standing watch by a fountain. The knight's shield bore a bough of rowan berries. The knight told Relkin that an enchantress named Calendria *had cursed the fountain so its waters became a green wine so sweet and intoxicating any who drank from it forgot their wits and fell into eternal slumber. When Relkin asked how to break the spell the knight told the prince,* "You must kill me and throw me in the fountain." *Reluctantly, Relkin did so and as soon as the rowan knight's body sank beneath the water the sleepers who drank from the bewitched fountain were freed from their curse. As they awoke they told Relkin they had shared a dream in which they were stoking a tower of fire that reached to the sky. The dreamers said they fed the flames of the tower by adding kindling made from their memories and knowledge. This tower of fire was the source of Calendria's power. Relkin found the enchantress, a maiden dressed in green hiding beneath a willow, now helpless without her magic. He ran her through with his sword.*

Thelonious considered the story again. The tower of fire in the dream reminded him of the Library. In a way, it too was a tower that contained the minds of all his countrymen in the form of books. He returned to the diary. As he studied the pages more closely he almost leapt out of his chair. All at once the heavy swirls of ink looked like old acquaintances: punctuation dotted with black smudges as from tiny cannonballs; the wispy flourish on the ends of letters like fox tails. He recognized the handwriting. Everything about it practically shouted the name "Ascalon Brown." His old mentor wrote this diary with the Rowan Knight as his pen-name! He took that to imply that he, like the character, was also a guardian of answers. If proven true, his diary would expose the Evening King as the greatest hoax in living memory. Thelonious flipped ahead in the diary.

A quiet groundswell of opposition is on the rise. Freethinkers all over Brander, working class men and women, are organizing, discussing the false religion of the Clockwork, our social disorder and the abuse of the Cabinet. Our goals are reasonable though far from simple. We demand freedom of education so that books, reading and writing may be enjoyed by all and not just the privileged few; freedom to represent ourselves in a parliament of the people; equality between rich and poor to lower the tax burden; and a swift end to the cycle of worker oppression so that fair wages and decent housing will save the laborer from a lifetime of enslavement.

Thelonious felt roused by these words. His foster father's lifework truly had been giving poverty-stricken people the same chance he had given an abandoned boy from the factories.

The newspapers have branded these freedom fighters "Black Cats" due to the deadly "accidents" they incite in protest. Their meetings are conducted with the utmost secrecy. In order to gain entry one must present oneself at Armory Square in the Wormwood Quarter, between the hours of three and four. Wait by the lamppost with a black handkerchief worn in your breast pocket. That is the signal. If they deem you trustworthy, one of their operatives will contact you saying, "Learn Forever", *to which you must respond,* "Yield Never." *That is the password. The truth is the Library's Room of Answers…*

The last page had been torn out. Dr. Dropwort's words came back to him: the professor's body found in the street with a black handkerchief dropped nearby. So it was true. Prof. Brown had been involved with the Black Cats. How else could he have gleaned such insight into their covert affairs? This diary amounted to a confession. Prof. Brown, lured by the Cats' talk of liberation, secretly aided them in their mission to protect the downtrodden. As secretary for the Bal Cypress Club they must have thought there was no limit to the amount of information he could have fed them with the contents of the Library at his disposal: books, maps, city records, private plans of high ranking Cabinet Ministers. Had he met their leader, this Paradise Street Dynamiter? Who knows how deep he'd gone. Yet for all his idealistic principles they repaid him with murder. Thelonious shut the diary, fist clenched on the cover. Like the professor, he too would track down these so-called "freedom fighters", gain their trust, penetrate their inner circle and find the man responsible for killing the only person who ever cared for him. If the Black Cats claimed to be working for the good of the people but were capable of shedding innocent blood then they really were just mindless fanatics like Dropwort said. Thelonious determined to bring his grievance down on their leader's head, expose them for the liars and criminals they were and, if possible, exact his vengeance.

CHAPTER FOUR
MASTER OF THE YELLOW COURT

From Bal Cypress' *Preludium Collected Verse From the Forty Corners: Provinces of Praddingford, Malchire, Cumberwold, Greychester and others*

Once in the Forty Corners a cotter and his wife lived near a dark forest. One day the cotter's wife went to the oven to fetch a loaf of brown bread she'd been baking. She opened the oven to find the bread had become a plum cake full of brandied currants and sugared almonds. Curious things continued to happen around their house. When she woke in the morning her coarse, wool blanket carried the scent of exquisite perfume. Outside, the weeds around her door became a garden of colorful flowers. When she washed her dress in the laundry tub her plain rags became a ballgown of purest silk sewn with silver thread and studded with diamonds. This went on until one night a mysterious stranger knocked at their door. He wore a white waistcoat that was ripped and filthy. His hair was overgrown and scraggly as a rat's nest. His fingernails were long and sharp as rusty knives. He introduced himself as "Mr. Wildboots" saying he'd come with a message from the "Master of the Yellow Court." He informed the cotter and his wife that their house was on his master's land which made them his subjects. He said they must leave at once or swear fealty to the Master of the Yellow Court. The cotter objected saying he'd built this house with his own hands years ago without ever hearing of any lord in these parts, thank you very much. Wildboots replied a single stone in the corner of their house was from the foundations of his master's castle which once stood on this spot, therefore the house and all its inhabitants were part of his master's domain. The cotter told the hairy gentleman to get off his property and never return.

"You've eaten his food and accepted his hospitality," said Wildboots, "He will collect what is owed him."

The cotter warned his wife they mustn't accept anymore magical gifts the house provided. So they lived surrounded by sweet desserts and rich finery, miserable as the day is long because they couldn't enjoy it. In the fullness of time the cotter's wife conceived and was with child. She gave birth to a wretched monster covered in fur. As soon as it was born it leapt from its cradle to scream, "I must away to my father, Master of the Yellow Court!"

The creature snatched up the cotter's wife and flew out the window with her, never to be seen again. Belief in etherials still runs strong in the Forty Corners. Cornermen are given to marvelous tale-telling and quaint superstitions. They say the Giant Anic once washed away an entire village with a flood of his piss and those who survived rebuilt their homes as the city of Brander. Prince Relkin is said to be buried in the Cornerlands somewhere in the shadow of Mount Horn among the common folk he loved better than his own family. Ancient stone circles dot the hillsides. Unknown symbols are carved in trees. Ancient artifacts –swords, rings, armor– turn up in plowfields or under hedges. They say there are men who converse with owls or girls who turn into cats. Hot springs with healing properties are rumored to be found at the bottom of hidden ravines. Old family names still survive such as "Moonborn", "Birdwhistle" and "Drinkwine." Locals claim to hear music in the air, voices in the night or notice strange lights in the sky.

A comprehensive study of the creatures was recorded by Ms. Prunella Allgood *in her book* On The Etherials: Darkling Cousins, Misbegotten of the Giant Anic. *She writes "the etherian temperament is fickle, vain and spiteful. Forever lovers of making bargains, their nimble cunning is only employed in trickery and deceit for pursuit of ends incomprehensible to mortals." Allgood began work on the subject when she first encountered one of their race as a girl. Wandering far from home, picking flowers, she saw a lady in a rainbow gown made of butterflies.*

"What pretty eyes you have!" said the lady, "May I have one?" With that, she plucked young Allgood's left eyeball from its socket, heedless of the child's screams and stood admiring her bloody prize as Allgood ran, half-blind, back to her parents.

"They cannot be reasoned with," she later wrote, "They have no concept of pain, sickness, age or even death. The enmity between our peoples when my grandfather made war on them has long been considered the source of their ill will toward us. I do not believe that is the case. They are creatures born of madness. They can no more identify the notion of 'friend' anymore than 'foe.' The Lady In the Butterfly Dress did not steal my eye as retribution for crimes our people waged against hers. Just as I was picking flowers, she tore out my eye because she liked the color. These creatures were never at war with us. From their perspective we have always been, at best, objects of curiosity."

Over the course of her life Allgood compiled many firsthand accounts of similarly bizarre events. She tells of a Mr. Butterberry from the village of Parlan's Field who, while walking home one night down a familiar country road, suddenly found himself a guest at a magnificent banquet hosted by a man in a yellow tailcoat. After enjoying the raucous party with talking animals in attendance, Mr. Butterberry announced he must set off for home. This offended his host who implored him to stay, but Butterberry insisted the hour was late and he must get to bed. So the man in yellow bid him leave, assuring him "no one will harm you." Lost in the dark, Mr. Butterberry was attacked and eaten by three giant black dogs. One can only infer the name of these beasts was "No One." Other stories include a beautiful virgin who was kidnapped before her wedding by nine sisters who forced her to take a scalding hot bath every night until she turned into an ugly, withered crone. A miller's son who played at casting dice and other games of chance with merry youths under a hill and won a sack of gold only to return home to find fifty years had passed and everyone he knew was gone. A foolish lord who invited an etherian ruler to tea in hopes to gain the creature's favor. He and all his household met disastrous fates, unable to leave the mansion ever again. One etherial waged war against another, a ruler of a place called "Dreamfruit." After he conquered his rival's land by turning him to peppermint, he renamed it "Thereafter Blue." When asked why he destroyed so many of his cousins he replied, "I just couldn't stand that name." Then there are reports of etherials stealing babies.

Allgood explains etherials were not created, therefore they cannot create. Hence they are unable to bear children of their own. It is also why they are so fond of making deals with mortals. Everything they are is illusion and artifice from the gifts they bestow to the titles they inhabit. So in order to gain servants, treasure or power they must borrow and cheat through oaths and covenants. This calls into question the origin of Prince Relkin's magic sword Beautiful which was sharp enough to sever the cord of death and return a person to life. An etherian object, they must have stolen it from somewhere but from whom remains a mystery. The irony of such a blade which saved so many couldn't be used by Relkin on himself once he was dead. Allgood notes etherials have a drastic aversion to metal which is possibly why they are so seldom seen these days in our modern cities. Allgood posits that most of Relkin's adventures in the Forty Corners actually took place in the etherian realms, collectively known as the Dwellance, *as he is one of the few men to emerge unscathed from interactions with their kind.*

Below is a list of etherials said to reside in the region:

Gossamer Tangle – "Master of the Yellow Court", "His Gilded Grace", "Keeper of A Hundred Keys", "Squire of the Broken Mirror", "Riddlemaker", "Old Nocturne", "Dimber- Damber", "Onion Isaac", "M'Lady's Truefriend", "Herald of Oak, Ash and Thorn", an etherian ruler, arrogant, moody, seductive. Tangle is said to preside over the City of Birds, the Sea of Wine, the Glass Mountain, the Iron Brambles, Kingdom of Half-A-Summer and many other fanciful places.

John Marmalade – red eyes, eats children, once a rival ruler, now deposed by Tangle

Wildboots – long teeth, fingernails and hair with a weakness for rum

Tea-For-Two – his song drives people to suicide

The Jennyweed – a human woman captured by Tangle

Mudpie – web footed, web fingered

Fairest Goldthread – half man/half woman

Pumpkineater – steals from lonely travelers, fascinated by manmade objects, his heart is a hollow gourd where he stashes his trinkets

Melancholia
Trill
Chamomile
Porcelain
Diaphany } Tangle's nine beautiful but cruel daughters
Alas
Harpsichord
Mayapple
Euphonia

Cackletub – his daughters' governess, her tears are laudanum
Thimble and Snapdragon – his daughters' footmen

CHAPTER FIVE
THE PARADISE STREET DYNAMITER

Thelonious waited beneath the lamppost in the center of Armory Square. The lanterns on its sculpted limbs forked out like iron branches on a black tree. As instructed, he'd worn a black handkerchief in his top pocket. He paced nervously back and forth. The square was a bustle of commotion. Possibly why it was chosen as the appointed hour; plenty of faces to get lost in. He noticed a Scarlet Guard leaning against a brick wall polishing his musket. If they even suspected what he was doing he'd be flung in a Bellrath dungeon or worse. He pretended to blow his nose, moving the handkerchief into obvious visibility, then dropped it to his side fearing he'd overplayed his hand and alerted suspicion. No one seemed to take any notice of him as they shuffled past. What if the Black Cat agent missed him in the crowd? What if the tiny, dark fabric couldn't be seen among all the other drab and dirty clothing pressed around him? Feeling sick, in need of a drink, he wished this was over and done with. Across the street stood the Drollery; pleasure palace for the idle rich where men from all over the city went to indulge its decadent amusements. Prostitution was a perilous avenue fraught with violence and disease and many turned to houses of ill repute rather than trawl the streets alone. The Drollery was still a brothel however up-market its appearance. The outer wall was high and fortified. Inside decorative pillars upheld tiered balconies with hanging gardens like an opera house. Lavish courtyards lined with gambling tables, steam baths, massage parlors and a nightly masquerade where indolent sons of noble birth could frolic in the paid company of painted women before retiring to a comfortable suite. There were also, on the lower levels, accommodations for customers of smaller purse where a night of cheap rum with a haggard wench in rough barracks could be bought for five coppers. Thelonious shuddered. The only life worse than a boy in the factories was a girl in the Drollery, whether she was a courtesan dancing in its gilded ballroom or a hapless waif thrown to lewd scoundrels in its dank cellar. "Little filth! Out of the way!" Fearing the Scarlet Guard, Thelonious spun around to see a small paperboy with black smudges on his cheeks and a bundle of newspapers slung over his shoulder. A fat man pushing a cart of chimney brushes swatted at the boy with a rolled up copy of *The Brander Gazette*. "But sir!" the child pleaded, "That's one copper!"

"Piss off!" the fat man shouted, pushing on with his cart, nearly running the boy over. Thelonious took a step in the man's direction then froze. He couldn't risk starting trouble and draw attention to himself. He looked at the little urchin and felt overcome with pity. "Here," he said handing the boy a copper in payment. The boy smiled, "Learn forever," he mumbled, barely audible above the surrounding noise. Thelonious was so surprised he nearly forgot his response. "Yield never," he replied.

The boy glanced over his shoulder and pulled his cap further down. "The Green Maiden on Paradise Street," he said in a raised whisper and with that, he shoved off through the crowd and was out of sight before Thelonious realized their brief interaction was over. Could it really be so simple? With but a word a trapdoor to the hidden world of anarchists had opened before him allowing passage if he dared. He pictured an ill-lit room in the back of some smoky tavern full of wild-eyed thieves and murderers, absinthe-drinkers, opium-eaters, their minds ravaged by corruption, sharpening their knives with devious laughter. Paradise Street. He should have known this path could only lead him back to that infernal bottom-end of the city. He remembered the choking smell of burning coal; the fetid heaps of trash, dead rats and rotting sewage that lined the cobbles. His fingers clumsily felt for the dagger stashed in his coat pocket like five little drunks. He steeled his resolve against impending dread. The answer to whatever befell Prof. Brown in his final hours lurked somewhere in his old life and if he intended to confront that place again he'd come prepared to fight. Wrapping his fingers around the tiny hilt Thelonious willed his feet in the direction of the Wormwood Quarter and its foul, looming cloud of smog that perpetually blackened half the sky. The Green Maiden was a small, ramshackle tavern easy to miss in the dingy squalor. Its squat, brown-shingled gable slumped to one side, half fallen in. Its crude, stone walls glistened with a nautical-looking algae. A pack of mangy dogs fought over a hen bone in a heap of oily rags outside the front door. Someone had carved a childish rhyme on the wall:

boom said the man on paradise street
boom says every man paradise on every street

Inside among the raucous singing of factory workers clinking tankards of ale at long rough-hewn tables and benches arranged around a wide, stone fireplace, a cauldron of onions, leeks and parsnips boiled over the logs. Heavy ship's ropes hung from hooks on the walls. Wooden barrels were stacked in one corner. Burly, bearded men in soot-stained coveralls sat around eating simple meals of sausage, bread and bowls of thin, watery soup. An old woman in a stained apron hunched over the pot, ladling out bowlfuls while a serving girl carried them to tables with a pitcher, refilling drinks and picking up empty plates. As Thelonious navigated the room, trying to look inconspicuous, he noticed one man, the biggest chap he'd ever seen with a messy red beard. He was tearing at a leg of mutton, wiping his mouth with a black handkerchief.

"May I join you?" asked Thelonious.

The big man eyed him warily. "Shove off, fancy lad!"

Thelonious knew he couldn't very well ask the man's political affiliation outright so he decided to venture a risky gambit.

"Learn forever?" he tried.

The big man scowled at him. "What did you say?" He pushed away from the table and stood up. "You call me stupid?"

Thelonious realized suddenly, with mounting panic that the big man's handkerchief was just an ordinary white handkerchief, long unwashed, darkened by grease. "I think it's about time someone kick you and your fancy clothes back to where you belong!"

As Thelonious braced himself another young man stepped between them. He wore a heavy, tweed overcoat, brown trousers with suspenders and a flat cap. He was taller than Thelonious with a flushed, lumpen face, round cheeks and a meager hope of blonde hairs above his upper lip.

"There you are!" the young man greeted the big man cheerfully. "Gettin' on alright? I see you've met me cousin here!" He turned to Thelonious. "Where've you been? We've been lookin' all over for you!"

Before the big man could react the young man took Thelonious by the shoulder and steered him away toward other side of the tavern. "Thanks," Thelonious whispered. "I assume you're the person I've come to see?"

"Alec Stove," the young man introduced himself sitting them down at a table near the fire with a few other men seated around them. They nodded at him with icy reserve.

"Fellows," said Alec to the group. "Seems we've a new prospect joining us for supper. A mister…"

"Rowan."

"Well, Mr. Rowan," said the one called Alec. "You knew where to find us. You knew our signal. Who sent you?"

"No one," said Thelonious. "I work at the Library Tower."

"Oo, get him!" one man mocked. "Want a prize, do ya?"

"I beg your pardon?"

"We don't need his soft-heeled sort coming around here," the man continued. "Snobs, that's what they are! Hoarding all the books as if the secret to read makes them a damned sorcerer. Nobody gives a wet fart what some dead geezers wrote down!"

"I didn't mean to offend-"

"In me grandda's day libraries used to *lend* books, y'know. Old man near his home was village scribe. Mind you, it were no Three Marys. Only had nine, maybe ten books in all, but he gave 'em out to whoever asked. Not no more. Not after Mendle got hold of 'em. Might as well feed books to swine as far as they're concerned. Don't want us pauper's fingers smudging the pages, eh?"

Thelonious didn't know how to respond. "I…I read about the Black Ca…your associates…and was curious to see for myself." The men looked from one to the other.

"Do we trust him?" asked one in a low growl.

"For now," Alec winked at the others. "If his story proves unconvincing he won't get far."

Thelonious noticed many furtive glances cast in his direction from other tables. He began to appreciate the gravity of his situation. If he made a run for it a dozen ruffians would be on him before he reached the door. People disappeared every day in this part of town. The serving girl appeared at his elbow. "Anything to drink?" she demanded.

"Ellie!" Alec called the barmaid, "Ale for our guest!" before Thelonious could answer. "Absinthe," Thelonious corrected.

"Don't look so solemn," Alec chided him. "As they say, 'a big heart needn't fear a little rope!'" Thelonious tried to sip his drink with his quavering hand. Alec leaned back in his chair. "Now then, why does a bright fellow such as yourself want to join up with the likes of us?"

"I've read things in the Library. History doesn't make sense. The Clockwork. The Evening King. Everything is built on secrets and lies. If the Evening King's reign is illegitimate it should be exposed. I mean, are we to believe our country's been ruled by a century-old man sitting up in that castle, all the while unseen?"

"I supposed you believe the Evenking's an etherial in disguise and all that flummery?" one of the men laughed.

"Wouldn't mind that. Be like the good ol' days of jolly Queen Viv," someone piped in.

"Nursery tales!" another added. "Fie on that family and its petty wars!"

"Aye, when Morningtides waltz you don't pick the tune. But a few bonfires don't seem so bad after what followed. After her 'twas all left to Meddlin' Mendle and his blasted Evenking. Things took a right distasteful turn then, eh?"

Another man with rotten teeth shook his head. "I'd settle for a decent wage! I toiled for years in the Foundry. Once I got the bloody lung they turned me out on me arse."

"I got seven mouths at home," said another. "When I stole bread to fill hungry bellies they branded me with this," a scar in the shape of a "T" for "thief " was burned onto the back of his hand, "After that I couldn't get no work."

"I were a soldier," said another. "Went off to fight with the Scarlet Guard. Help drive them ill-men from our shores. Came back to find my wife had taken another man who'd taken my job."

Alec picked at a splinter in the table thoughtfully. "We all have our reasons for being here, Mr. Rowan."

"I can help you," said Thelonious. "I have access to documents. Proof of-"

"We need weapons, cannons, firepower!" said another irritably. "We don't need someone to write our enemies a letter!"

"What about the one they call the Paradise Street Dynamiter?" An uncomfortable hush fell about the table. "He supplies you with plenty of firepower, does he not?"

Alec cleared his throat. "Well now, meet some of the lads! That there's the Dawkins boys, ship's carpenters. Young Lucas here, baker's son. Mr. Chilson, tanner. This is Pip-"

"You look familiar," said Thelonious. "Haven't I seen you at the Library Tower?" He noticed his tongue was loosening. The effects of the drink.

"Sebastian Prentice," Pip explained. "My grandfather is Sir Pritchard."

"Ah yes, now I see the resemblance. You write for the *Gazette*." Alec stood up to address the table. "Alright, let's put it to a vote then, shall we?"

"Vote? On what?" Thelonious asked.

"On whether or not to let you stay," replied Alec.

"Whether or not to let you *leave* is more like," one muttered.

Thelonious looked Alec in the eye. "You're him, aren't you? This Dynamiter the whole city's looking for?"

The serving girl returned, wiping the table in front of him. He glanced down at the black handkerchief in her hand. Thelonious' head shot upright.

"A vote won't be necessary, boys," said the barmaid in a low tone. "Everyone out. I want a private word with our new recruit, Mr. Rowan here. Or do you prefer 'Mr. Brown?'"

As the men slowly rose and filed out Thelonious studied this woman for the first time. He never suspected this unassuming servant quietly attending her duties was the leader of an anarchist uprising; the architect behind the worst string of bombings Brander had ever seen. How long had she been listening to their conversation? Slipping unnoticed from table to table, refilling cups, surveying the entire room from a position of anonymity.

Alec patted her shoulder as he left. "Just give us the signal."

She was of average height, short mud-brown hair, a pinched nose and eyes the color of smoke, dressed in tan breeches, high black boots and a ruffled tunic.

"So you're the one," said Thelonious as she sat across from him. "You destroyed those factories."

Ellie didn't smile. "And you're Secretary for the Bal Cypress Club. Professor Ascalon's charge." "Did you know him?"

"Did we kill him you mean?"

Thelonious was taken aback. "Why would you ask a thing like that?"

"You haven't stopped fingering that blade in your pocket since you came in," she said.

Thelonious looked away.

"I've done you a kindness, Mr. Brown. Sparing you a vote. Majority would've called you unfit for our ranks. Would've voted to kill you. You might have taken a swing with that silly letter-opener of yours and they'd strike you down."

"Then you admit it?" asked Thelonious. "You Cats murder anyone who becomes a nuisance?"

Ellie smiled without mirth. "Your professor had enemies far worse than scullery maids. He was an aristocrat who raised a young guttersnipe. Spoke out against inequality. Traitor to his class."

Thelonious felt his face flush. "What are you saying?"

"I'm saying like all clever men of the world your cleverness will be your undoing." She sighed and took a sip from his cup of absinthe. "When will you intellectuals learn that scribbling in your precious diaries changes nothing?"

Thelonious gasped. "You left it for me, didn't you? The diary. At Hob's Inn."

"Of course! Waste of time, grown man writing notes like a schoolboy. Action is what counts."

"Without knowledge there can be no action."

"That another of your professor's sayings?"

"No, actually it was Humphrey Throckmorton who said—"

She raised her hand with an operatic flourish, "*Ward ye well this fortune read, empires none upon history tread that rival the splendors in thy head.*"

Thelonious sat stunned. He couldn't believe an uneducated barkeep could quote Throckmorton. "Only a handful of literary scholars at the Academy are familiar with that poem," said Thelonious. "How did you come by that line?"

She laughed bitterly. "What? My mouth not high and mighty enough to hold your pretty words? You think there's anything found in a book what can't be learned elsewhere?"

"Sebastian," Thelonious recalled. "Sir Pritchard's grandson. That's where you learned it. He could've snuck you Library books to study."

"Might be. But you have it the other way round. Sebastian needed us."

"Why?"

"Sir Pritchard's uncles, Leopold and Oliver Prentice, were a pair of book publishers during Queen Vivian's reign. A month after the Evening King's Cabinet took office they were ordered to close. Stop printing books. They refused. Days later their shop, Prentice Press, was raided by the Scarlet Guard. They were arrested and taken to Bellrath Prison, never to be heard from again." She paused. "You're seeing green, aren't you?"

"Excuse me?"

"Inebriety. Absinthe sickness. I can tell." Thelonious stood up angrily. A firm hand on his shoulder shoved him down again. "Please," he whimpered. "If you mean to kill me, first I must find the man who killed the professor."

"Don't fret," Ellie reassured him. "You're alive because you're useful." She jerked her head at Alec. Within moments all the men gathered back at the table.

"Good news, boys," she announced. "Our friend here has agreed to join our cause. So now would be time to go over tomorrow night." She held up a small vial of a clear, gel-like compound.

"What is it?" someone asked.

"My own invention. A new weapon."

"In that little bottle?" it was one of the Dawkins boys who spoke.

"A chemical incendiary agent."

"A what?" Dawkins asked.

"Bomb," Alec cut in.

"Not strictly speaking," said Ellie. "More like liquid fire."

Dawkins' face was still a thick blank. "How's it work then?"

"I read a research paper by Professor Lysander Scarabus on the alchemists in Ismere and Ilphane. They describe a mixture of quicklime, sulphur, resin and saltpeter."

Thelonious' eyebrows raised. "You're talking about pyromancy!" he exclaimed. "I took Prof. Scarabus' class at the Academy. He said the Elephant Emperor's court magicians used a sticky paste to scorch enemy ships. A substance they modified from barbarian raiders who threw hot tar and pitch…" He stopped when he realized everyone was staring at him.

Ellie grinned. "I've perfected their recipe."

"Made of what?"

"Distilled from compost."

"What, you mean dung?" Dawkins chuckled. "You invented explosive shit? Ho! That'll intimidate our enemies a fair treat!"

"Liquid fire," Ellie corrected. "Inextinguishable once lit. It burns even on water. In fact, water only spreads the flame. Makes it burn hotter."

Dawkins considered this. "I don't like it one bit! Sounds like sorcery to me!"

"Science," Ellie retorted.

"Hear her out," said Alec. "If we're to send the Cabinet a message, this concoction will be our envelope."

Dawkins shook his head. "Dynamite's one thing. I'm all for leveling factories. But this? Don't sound safe or natural."

"I must agree," said Thelonious. "It's incredibly volatile. By Prof. Scarabus' account even the alchemists had their apprentices mix and transport the substance because so many of them were burned alive while preparing it."

"I've taken every precaution," Ellie assured them. "I have nine barrels hidden below us in the cellar. That should be enough."

Enough to reduce half the city to a cinder, thought Thelonious, feeling increasingly anxious.

"What's our target then?" someone asked.

"The Drollery."

The men began to mutter amongst themselves. "You must be joking!" shouted Lucas. "No way in unless you've coin to pay. A redbreast at every door."

"And for what?" Dawkins added. "Just to fry a few dandies with their trousers down?"

Ellie stood. "The Drollery is a symbol for how the rich take pleasure from our pain. They treat our wives, mothers and daughters as playthings. How many women are debtors locked in that velvet cage? Kidnapped, sold or driven by hardship into their beds only to be thrown to early graves when they get bored. How many of you have children? Mr. Chilson, your daughter, how old is she? Eleven? Twelve? How long can she sell matchsticks barefoot in the snow? How long until some lecherous noble casts an appraising eye on her? What choices will she have then? I say we burn that place to the ground!"

The men were quiet for some time.

"We're no gallants in shiny armor, you know," Dawkins grumbled. "We do this, we're bound to end up like poor Raggedy Jack…with no use for a hat."

"I knew Jack," said Ellie softly. "Though that wasn't his real name.

The Rag Jack Resistance failed because they fought honorably. Abided by the rules of war, out in the open on a soldier's terms. That was their mistake. We, on the other hand, move in the darkness. Attack unseen. Cutting our enemies' legs out from under them one by one."

"I don't much like this, Elle," said old Chilson. "But you've helped me and mine, so I'm with you."

"And me," added Lucas.

One by one, the other men voiced their support. "What the hell,"

Dawkins grumbled. "A man only dies once."

Ellie turned to Thelonious, "Follow me, Mr. Brown." And Thelonious, not sure any longer if he had a choice, followed the leader of the Black Cats.

CHAPTER SIX
THALANA & THE MEN OF CLAY

From Bal Cypress' *Preludium*

Once in his travels Prince Relkin came upon the village of Blackthorpe in the Forty Corners. The townsfolk were troubled by men made of earth who came up out of the ground to clog their town's wells with rocks. Investigating the holes nearby, Relkin fell through to the underground city of Dar Daleric *where he met* Draluke, *leader of the mudmen. "Why are you choking the wells of the people above?" asked* Relkin, *"They need that water to survive." And Draluke explained, "As do we. Our race was created by an auldenarch, same as yours. The auldenarchs are not infallible as they would have us believe. There are mistakes in all their work. Our maker was* Thalana, *the sixth auldenarch, who formed us by accident out of wet clay. A lover of ceramics, Thalana dwelt in a cave deep beneath the mountains where she worked with her hands to craft urns and bowls. One day, bored with her work, she spat into the depths of her cave forming a great pool of mud. Reaching down, she sculpted dolls from this mixture which she intended to keep as playthings and left them to harden beside her fiery kiln. When she returned and saw her empty vessels risen to life, walking upright, she tried to smash them in disgust. But the mudmen cried out in fear for her to spare them and Thalana took pity on her creations. She named us* dwurmen *and gave us her underground world to inhabit. But she made us imperfect. Our bodies are fragile, hollow, given to dry and crack. So we must return each year to the cave where Thalana wet the earth and immerse ourselves in the* Pool of Dunya, *reborn in darkness or else crumble to dust. Those wells above draw from this Pool, our shared womb, draining it of the life-giving waters we need to sustain our mortal form." Relkin returned to the upper world and brokered a treaty between the villagers and the dwurmen. In exchange for closing the wells which led to the sacred Pool, the dwurmen agreed to help the villagers dig new wells further from the town. But the villagers of Blackthorpe were hard-hearted. "Why should we go miles out of our way to carry heavy bucketloads when we have fresh springs beneath our feet? Besides, these mudmen are more pottery than people! Let them find a new sty in which to wallow!" Once the villagers learned that the dwurmen's clay flesh was easily broken and their underground city was laden with precious stones, the villagers attacked the dwurmen. Relkin tried to stop them but they wouldn't listen. Relkin fled the angry throng and descended into Dar Daleric to warn Draluke and his people to escape. But he found no mudmen in their city beneath the earth. All of them were gone. Vanished forever into the Pool of Dunya.*

CHAPTER SEVEN
BONFIRE WALTZ

"Let me explain to you the way of the world, Mr. Brown," said Ellie, fastening the door behind them as they headed out into the slanted alley. "Law and crime are one in the same. Two masks for the same face. Both terms are meaningless. The only thing that matters is privilege. Who does the naming. For when a man robs a house he is a thief but when he robs a nation he is a banker."

Ellie's gaze was far away as she led them through the winding backstreets. "I was born here," she said after a pause. "In a room over a cannery near Lower Grimstoke."

"Mungfish Tin Company?"

"That's right. I forgot, you grew up in this piss-pot too. That makes us neighbors, you and I. My father worked his whole life in the Plumbum Foundry. Dangerous work. Till one day there was an accident with the smelter. A leak ruptured in the tank dousing him with molten lead. Melted his flesh in an instant."

Thelonious shivered. For the second time since reading the professor's diary he felt sympathy, a kind of kinship with their cause.

"That's why you bombed it," he murmured. "To destroy the place that destroyed your father."

Ellie picked up a dagger hidden behind a stack of crates as if it had been left there for her and slid it in her belt. "That's when I became the Dynamiter. If the world had no use for good men like my father then I had no use for the world."

"Your hatred cost hundreds of other good men their livelihoods."

"There is no life in the factories!" she snapped. "You of all people know that." She paused by a heap of broken glass before continuing. "My mother was a Cloth Row seamstress until she lost her fingers in a loom. When they turned her out on the street she refused to sell herself to the Drollery. She worked alone. Endured ridicule as a 'fallen woman.' Until one night a rich boy refused her payment. When she fought back he struck her to death with his cane."

Thelonious turned up his collar against the first drops of rain.

"We are worthless to them," said Ellie. "Disposable parts so long as we serve our function. But the moment our bodies break, the moment we stand up for our rights, we're cast aside. We harvest their grain, manufacture their clothes, produce the goods they sell. It's time we remind them that *we* are the Clockwork they're so bloody fond of! The engine of progress, the ones who move society forward! Without us they could not survive."

Under a tangle of rusty steam pipes jutting from a wall she reached down and picked up a burlap sack. Inside the bag was a bundle of fine clothes and a pair of masquerade masks.

"Here. Put this on," she instructed, handing him one of the masks with gold-and-white stripes and a formal frock coat made of purple velvet. Ellie pulled a green dress on over her clothes and a frightening black mask with pointed ears. The metal filigree gate of the Drollery rose in the distance. "Alright," said Ellie. "Remember the plan."

A group of colorfully dressed entertainers came frolicking through the fog toward a half-dozen Scarlet Guards posted in front of the gate. There were jugglers, acrobats, fiddlers, puppeteers, some in red tights, pointy shoes, feathered caps with ribbons and bells, chatting amongst themselves, singing merrily. Ellie and Thelonious, behind their masks and gaudy attire, joined the milling throng of performers. The soldiers frisked them for weapons. Ellie's dagger went unnoticed concealed in the bodice of her dress. Once the gate was opened they were ushered inside a marble courtyard full of trickling fountains that dispensed red wine, tables laid with jam tarts and fruit. Men and women in fantastical garb glided arm-in-arm past fire-eaters, sword-swallowers, snake-charmers. Thelonious saw dancing in a ballroom beyond. By now Alec, Dawkins and the rest of the men would be loading the barrels into the lower level. Ellie bribed the guards to let them smuggle in her liquid fire under the pretense the crates were filled with absinthe for the party. Ellie told Thelonious that they would enter through the front disguised as actors and meet with the Drollery's madam whom she'd contacted earlier. The plan was simple: at the stroke of twelve the girls would place a sleeping draught in the men's cups and once their drunken customers had nodded off, they'd evacuate the building before the liquid fire was ignited. Ellie took his arm as they strolled through the chamber, completing the pose of a young couple attending a dance.

"Why yes," one man in the crowd was overheard bragging.

"My friends in the Cabinet have invested in my latest invention."

"What damn fool gadget have you cooked up for us this time, old boy?"

"A more efficient means of execution," said the man. "The warden at Bellrath Prison calls it a miracle of modern science."

"Quite, quite, I'm sure. What is it then?"

"I call it a 'lightning chair.'"

"Oh, I don't like the sound of that!" one woman gasped.

"How does it work?"

"The chair is electrified. Inlaid with pure silver for conductivity. The prisoner is restrained with leather straps around the wrists and ankles as a powerful current, fifty times stronger than my arklights, is sent jolting through his body, top to toe."

"Really Ben, it's simply ghastly!"

"How fiendishly clever!"

"Within a year it'll put the hangman out of business."

Ellie steered Thelonious away. "Pompous bastard," she whispered. "All that education gone to waste dreaming up new ways to kill us quicker."

Thelonious tried to change the subject. "So where is the…lady of the house?"

"Not yet," said Ellie in a hushed tone. "Try to blend in. Have a drink."

Thelonious shot her a glance, unsure if she meant that as a slight. At a table another group of nobles sat around playing some kind of board game he'd seen boys in his dormitory play once. On a round board of spiral, black-and-white tiles each player had a set of sixteen polished tokens, one set of ivory, the other of ebony. He looked at the pieces: an elephant, a chariot, a crocodile, a monkey…

"Do you play?" someone asked. Thelonious glanced up at the head of the table where an older man in a silvery-blue mask was playing against a woman in a fluffy gown and pink mask.

"Oh, thank you, no," said Thelonious graciously. "Just watching."

"It's the latest thing," said the man in the blue mask. "Called *banékar*, which I'm told roughly translates to 'maze of squares.'"

"It's only just arrived from Bael-Perazin," the woman added.

"Everything fashionable this season is." Thelonious nodded as the man who'd beckoned him continued to talk as he played.

"This war game," he explained, "was the sport of emperors for a thousand years. A lesson in strategy, each piece moves in a different way. The object is to maneuver your pieces around the circle. The first player to take the centermost square wins."

Thelonious thought the man looked oddly familiar even with half his face obscured. Something about that long nose and jutting ears. Thelonious slunk away from the table nervously. He was beginning to see spots before his eyes. Dark spots that opened into ugly, black flowers hovering in midair, their falling petals wilted in death. He shook his head but the hideous garden remained. *Absinthe hallucinations,* he thought, only now devoid of their usual gaiety, these were unsettling apparitions of madness and disease. Sweat beaded on his forehead as he closed his eyes, trying to will away the ghostly weeds.

"Upstairs," Ellie whispered in his ear. Without another word she rushed up the marble staircase toward the bedchambers on the floor above. Breathing heavily, Thelonious followed at a confused distance. For a place subject to such awful rumors, the Drollery did not fill him with revulsion as he thought it would. Save for the grotesque bouquet in his mind's eye, the party seemed pleasant enough. Then it struck him; why he recognized the old man at the gaming table. That voice. From his first day in the Library Tower. Osric Dropwort! The Lord-Regent of Anic, a guest of the Drollery at this debaucherous masquerade, drinking and gambling with prostitutes! Thelonious quickened his pace up the stairs after Ellie. On the second level was a long hallway lined with curtains. Murmurs hung in the air occasionally punctuated by a delighted squeal or rougher noises that sullied any illusion of elegance. A scream pierced one end of the hall. A moment later Ellie burst out a door dragging a girl in a white corset, kicking, flailing, from the bedroom. "No! You can't do this!" the girl screamed. "We must warn the others!"

"Hang the others!" Ellie replied, twisting the girl's arm. "There's no time!"

"This is monstrous, Elle!" wept the girl. "Even for you!"

Thelonious ran to them, uncertain how to react but fearful their row would attract attention.

"You think this is what mother would've wanted?" the girl demanded as Ellie bundled her toward the stairs.

"She'd want me to save you," said Ellie.

"But my friends!" the girl protested. "Nepenthe, Azalea, the other girls!"

"They couldn't be trusted."

"They don't deserve to die!"

Thelonious could barely form questions as he hurried to keep up. "Do you know who's downstairs?" he hissed.

"Dead men," Ellie replied.

"You can't kill a Cabinet Minister!"

Other curious faces in various states of undress began to peek from behind curtains as they sailed past.

"I won't let you do this!" the girl protested, just as a cry went up from below, "Fire! Fire!"

"It's done, Briar. We have to go," said Ellie, "Now."

The courtyard at the bottom of the stairs was filling with plumes of smoke as panicked crowds darted back and forth.

"Ellery!" an angry voice called from behind them.

They turned to see a Scarlet Guardsman, his musket aimed at Ellie. Through the chaotic haze Thelonious looked again at his companion as though for the first time.

"*Ellery*?" he repeated in astonishment.

"Give it up!" the soldier barked. "There's no escape! You're coming with me!"

"Idiot!" she spat. "Would you arrest me or live?"

Thelonious felt the heat rising from the floor beneath their feet. A troop of soldiers in red uniforms fell upon them, grabbing Ellie, the girl and Thelonious as a flaming pillar crashed around them.

CHAPTER EIGHT
THE EVENING KING

From Mendle's *Annals of the Kings of Anic, Vol. II:*

Over the course of her long and illustrious history Anic has known many eccentric rulers such as King Harrock the Dread who dug up his dead mistress and had his servants kiss her ring and wait on her at table; Blind King Tomothy who rode into battle lashed to his horse; King Leodain who once cooked a disrespectful lord into a pie; Queen Amaryllis a lover of animals who let deer, hedgehogs, toads and birds roam free inside her castle; Fardulf Flickwing the Bard King who renounced a life at court and traveled from town to town playing his lute; King Jonavan who clothed himself in ladies' dresses. I daresay when presented in the context of history we should not compare our beloved monarch, the Evening King, to the peculiar company of his predecessors. However few details about his personage can be revealed. The Library Tower offers the following assurances: He was born in the Forty Corners, the exact province is immaterial, but suffice it to say it was not far outside Brander. His ancestral lineage was verified through documents recovered from the Bookhouse at Three Marys and stored in the Library Tower for safekeeping. He is a distant but trueborn descendant of King Parlan.

CHAPTER NINE
WARD YE WELL THIS FORTUNE READ

A black spider skittered down the wet bricks to hover over a hand chained to the wall. In the deepest dungeon of Bellrath Prison Thelonious sat prodding a dirty plate of moldy bread left at his feet. He looked to his cellmate, the barmaid formerly known as Ellie, who sat examining the links on her own manacled wrist. After a restless night in this damp, stinking hole his exhaustion finally gave way to courage enough to confront her.

"*You're* Ellery Fathom?" he blurted.

She sighed. "You needn't sound so surprised."

"Surprised? It's unthinkable! A Cabinet Minister, Inspector General of the Scarlet Guard no less… also head of the Black Cats?"

Her mouth curved like a dagger into a forgery of a smile.

"How can one person live two lives so at odds? Your soldiers hunt anarchists. Your anarchists kill soldiers. How was this double-dealing not found out before?"

"As my father used to say to my brother, 'If your brains were dynamite you wouldn't have enough to blow your ears off.'"

Thelonious looked up as he heard keys jingle and rusty hinges creak as someone entered. Through the bars he saw a soldier approach he recognized from the night before. He rested an arm on the bars, staring at Ellery with a crooked grin.

"No escape this time, Elle," he said in a haughty tone. "None of your tricks will save you now. I've really caught you once and for all."

"You must be so pleased with yourself, Finn," Ellery taunted. "Always a happy lackey. Even as a boy. A natural follower. Never content without orders to obey. A master to serve. Mother would be proud."

The soldier slammed his hand against the cage. "Don't invoke her to shame me!" he shouted, a sudden flash of anger reddening his face. "She broke the rules, Elle, just like you! *That's* why she died." He looked away to compose himself. "A lesson, I'm sorry to see you still haven't learned."

Ellery gritted her teeth. "She broke the rules to put food in your ungrateful mouth."

He clucked bitterly.

"Where's Briar?"

"Far from you and your vile influence. Can't abide another scapegrace in the family."

"You know she had no part in this, Finn."

"On the contrary, I've taken a personal hand in our sister becoming a respectable lady."

Thelonious noted a livid rage rising behind Ellery's dark eyes.

"She's to marry Lord Melrose's son, Quinton. Not the most upstanding bachelor, I grant you, but he's just inherited his father's fortune and as a…patron of Briar's services in the past he's quite taken with her. Willing to overlook her career as a Drollery whore he's offered her a new beginning as nobleman's wife to ensure she won't fall back on her old ways. Not that there's much of that place left to revisit anyway after your fire."

"You'd take her from one prison to another," Ellery spat.

"We caught your friends, by the way. Those turnkeys and rat-catchers you consort with. One of them burnt to a crisp. Did you know that? Another was shot. The rest are in the next cell."

"Liar," she said quietly, sounding half-amused. "You never had a knack for it, Finn."

"Like you?"

Ellery met his gaze. "I'll stop you. I always do. I won't let you give Briar to some spoiled brat as her new warden."

"What I can't understand is how you keep getting away with it. Why no one ever believed me when I told them my sister is the Dynamiter of Paradise Street; that she betrayed her post again and again to attack the city she swore to protect. Do you have other friends in the Cabinet? A pardon from the Evening King?"

"That empty carriage, you mean?" Ellery countered, "The one they parade around the streets once a year to keep up the charade that someone's in charge?"

"More baseless accusations from those Black Cat malcontents you're so fond of!" Finn scoffed, "You haven't a shred of evidence to support such a ridiculous claim."

"Neither have you."

He squinted at her, puzzled.

"I am Lord-Magistrate," Ellery continued, "Inspector General of the Scarlet Guard, *your* commanding officer, defender of law and order. You can prove nothing to the contrary."

Finn snorted. "Why you of all people should even sully your tongue with these mad conspiracies when you've had audience with the king himself! You and the other ministers meet with him, talk to him, in person!"

Ellery smirked. "What makes you think it's a 'him'?"

Finn paced away from the cage to bridle his temper. "Fine. Have it your way, then. Keep your childish riddles! You do know you're to be executed tomorrow?"

Thelonious' eyes grew wide.

"Oh yes, you and your talkative accomplice as well," Finn added.

"Tomorrow is Midwinter's Eve," said Ellery calmly.

"And?"

"The anniversary of an end to the Morningtides' war and the beginning of a long evening that has not lifted these hundred years."

"A hundred years of peace and stability."

"And darkness," said Ellery. "Darkness that obscures the truth and hides cruelty done in plain sight. Darkness that clouds the minds of a people divided against themselves so men don't see their own hands around their brothers' throats, lest they awaken to the fact they're condemned to life. Tormented all their days poisoning the water they drink, the air they breathe, with no choice but to serve the greed of their oppressors. Because for so long you have refused to see the light we must burn down the world until there is no darkness left. 'Boom' says every man…"

"Enough!" shouted Finn.

"…paradise on every street," she whispered.

He clenched a gloved fist. "We have quaint phrases of our own," he warned. "Such as 'bow your head or part with it.' Like your lover, the Rag Jack, what was his name?"

Ellery clenched her jaw.

"You beheaded him yourself. I'll never understand why. If your plan was always revolution, why kill him and all his men?" Thelonious braced himself, ready for Ellery to strike.

"Or did his death spur your treacherous heart to finish what he'd started?" asked Finn.

"Tomorrow I'll show you."

Finn laughed. "Tomorrow that smug head of yours will finally leave its shoulders and *I* will be hailed as Brander's greatest savior."

"You have your job to do and so have I," said Ellery. "Time is a small matter."

With a final noise of disgust Finn turned and marched out the door. "No one in or out of this cell until I return, understand?" he barked at the two guards on watch. "Yes sir," they replied in unison. The heavy latch slammed shut behind him and Thelonious and Ellery were left in silence once again.

"I never should have trusted you," Thelonious moaned.

"I just gave you the diary. You chose to stick your nose in," Ellery replied. "You're here of your own accord, same as me."

"That soldier, your brother, he knows what you are! He'll give your whole game away!"

"A game he's lost many times before."

"Then if you won't tell him, tell me. How did the leader of the Black Cats become commander of the Scarlet Guard?"

Ellery picked at the lock on her wrist. "I supposed we're not going anywhere for a while," she sighed. "Alright then. A story to pass the time." She closed one eye as she worked, "After I lost my parents I disguised myself as a boy and worked as a pickpocket in the Blood Bowl. I learned I could make more money fingering other pickpockets and let the Guards round up my competition. It soon became a full time job. I worked my way up to professional thief-taker. With my know-how in the housebreaker business I single-handedly put almost every master thief in the Quarter behind bars. Then I discovered I could make more money if I played both sides. I released a few old colleagues from jail and cut a deal with them. They would rob wealthy pedestrians and bring their ill-gotten gain to me. The victims reported these crimes, describe what they'd lost and in a few days I would reunite them with their stolen items for a finder's fee. If they could not pay what we asked we'd fence the loot. Either way, I'd split the profit with my comrades and the cycle would repeat. Our gang took over other gangs and before long I was running a lucrative enterprise with even dozens in the Scarlet Guard on our payroll. It was three years before the Cabinet learned of corruption in its ranks. Lord Osric Dropwort sent Sir Cuthbert Margrave, the previous Lord-Magistrate, to investigate. I manipulated him into hiring me as an undercover informant, 'Inspector General' of his secret police. Believing I worked for them, I spent the next decade infiltrating the Cabinet's hierarchy with Black Cat agents of my own, all the while feeding them false information as to where we'd target next. When Sir Cuthbert died I took over his title as the new Lord-Magistrate."

"And the Rag Jack Resistance?" Thelonious asked hesitantly.

Ellery's gaze fell. "Such was my devotion to the role I played," she said after a pause. "If I didn't respond as Commander of the Scarlet Guard I knew I'd draw Dropwort's suspicion. I would have forfeited everything, years of planning, my people's future, all for the man I loved."

With a click, the lock on her wrist clattered to the ground.

"Come on," she instructed him, turning her attention to his manacles. In moments Thelonious was free as well as Ellery quickly picked the barred door of their cell.

"Brilliant!" whispered Thelonious. "But what about the guards?"

They found the heavy door to the hallway left unlocked and, before Thelonious could stop her, Ellery strode out into the open past the two watchmen who didn't move, didn't even blink, in acknowledgment of her presence. Thelonious was dumbfounded at their inaction. "How…?" he breathed.

Ellery cast them a disdainful smile over her shoulder, "Learn forever!" she called.

"Yield never!" they replied.

"Who ordered our release?" she asked.

"Captain Finnegan Fathom, ma'am."

"That's right." She led Thelonious through Bellrath's underg- round tunnels, past other cells full of beggars, rapists and lunatics, up and out of the dungeons and into daylight. At each checkpoint the guards moved aside and held open doors for them without a word.

"Bloody hell!" Thelonious exclaimed in relief once they were safely on their way along with the bustling crowds of Mercantile Lane. "Just how many Scarlet Guards are secretly Black Cats?"

"Enough," she said. "But most only know me as Inspector General and follow my orders without question."

"Where are we going?"

"The Library Tower."

"What for?"

"There is a book there, hidden. The one Three Marys was destroyed to conceal. The book which contains the Evening King's true identity."

"Nonsense! I tell you there is no such book! I should know, I was secretary."

"The missing page from your professor's diary," Ellery reminded him, "I removed it before I gave it to you. It was too important to fall into the wrong hands. That page tells how to find a secret room in the Library sealed off one hundred years ago when the Tower was first built."

"The Room of Answers?" Thelonious gasped.

"Inside are tens of thousands of manuscripts kept from public record."

"I knew it! I knew there had to be more!"

As they hurried through the butcher's markets and cabbage vendors they passed a throng of people buying papers from a newsstand with a boy crying the latest headline: "DROLLERY DESTROYED! DROPWORT DEAD! BLACK CATS DECLARE WAR!"

"This has gotten quite out of hand," Thelonious muttered. "Did you know he'd be there that night?"

"Who?"

"Dropwort."

"Yes."

"But why?"

"Masters are a tiresome business," said Ellery, "But I burned down the Drollery to rescue my sister."

"Brander will burn for this! You know that, don't you?" said Thelonious, sick with fear. "There will be open bloodshed in the streets! With the Lord Regent of Anic murdered, the violence on both sides will erupt!"

"Dropwort was the one who ordered the destruction of the Plumbum Foundry."

Thelonious shot her a glance. "You said your father died there in an accident…"

"True. But remember, I was just a thief who became a better thief, a Cabinet Minister. It was Dropwort's idea to use the rebellion of the poor for his own ends. Knowing my life's story, he tasked me with a secret mission: pose as an anarchist and destroy the factory that had caused my family such grief."

"Why would the Lord-Regent encourage such danger in his city?"

"He owned the Foundry. It was losing money. He could no longer afford to pay the workers' wages. So he had me get rid of it in a way that turned the blame on the Black Cats. And the Paradise Street Dynamiter was born."

Thelonious was speechless.

"I accepted because I knew he was offering me power that eventually he wouldn't be able to control. He didn't know he was putting fire, smoke, chaos itself into my hands." She wiped her mouth on the back of her sleeve. "The Drollery was my own doing, of course. I'd had enough of Dropwort; running his murderous errands. So I freed my sister –and myself– in one stroke."

They crossed Tollgate Bridge into the Quicksilver Quarter, down Leviathan & Hemlock to Nightshade & Papyrus until they reached the gray spire of the Library. Ellery took Thelonious by the shoulders. "Go up and knock," she instructed. "They'll recognize your face and open the door."

"I was dismissed," he informed her crossly. "And not on the best of terms. So I'm hardly a welcome visitor."

"Just get us inside and I'll handle the rest!"

Angry but out of excuses, Thelonious pulled the chain to ring the bell. A minute later the thunderous locks clunked and the doors began to move. Ellery ran forward and pushed through. Mr. Candlewick was knocked aside in a flurry of panic and wig powder,

"Mr. Brown!" he shouted, "What is the meaning of this intrusion?"

Thelonious ignored him and hurried up the stairs after Ellery.

"Young lady! Young lady! You can't go up there!" Candlewick called after her, but they were too far ahead to hear the rest. Ellery was already out of his sight as Thelonious bounded up the stone steps, three at a time, hoping to catch her as he rounded the next landing. When he reached the top he could already smell the acrid stench of burning paper. The room was full of smoke. There in the center, by the owl-legged table, stood Ellery, Anic's few precious bookshelves ablaze before her.

"What have you done?!" he screamed, horrified.

"My last vial of liquid fire," she explained. The grand painting of Bal Cypress above them began to melt and warp from the heat.

"How could you?!" he shrieked, short of breath from the effort.

She didn't respond. She didn't even look at him.

"But the book!" he wept. "The proof!"

"There is no book, you fool!" she snapped. "There is no Room of Answers! Even if there was there isn't one now!"

She took him by the arm and steered him toward the stairs but he wouldn't budge.

"No, the professor said…he said…"

"It was all a lie!" Ellery roared in frustration.

"No, the missing page! You said when you took the diary…" Thelonious' eyes locked on hers. The bottomless surge of emotions that roiled through his body was almost paralyzing.

"You?"

Ellery's expression held no remorse, no pity. Thelonious muttered helplessly, "You killed him!" The flames licked up the walls toward the green glass ceiling.

"Run!" Ellery commanded and they fled the burning Tower back down the way they'd come. Outside on the ground floor they were confronted by a troop of Scarlet Guards, aiming their muskets at them.

"Arrest that man!" Ellery ordered, pointed at Thelonious. "He's the Paradise Street Dynamiter!" Thelonious was too shocked to make a sound as the soldiers bound him by the hands and dragged him away from the smoking inferno high above.

That night, again in a dungeon deep below Bellrath Prison, Thelonious sat chained to the wall staring into the darkness, listening to the drip-drip-drip from cracks overhead. Drifting in and out of consciousness, his mind racing, he tried to make sense of the events of the day. Aching for absinthe, wild thoughts carried him swiftly down unpleasant corridors: *the loneliest, a Dogyard pup, Learn Foreverleague Academy, their Clockwork brains run on steam, a stone book with blank pages, Zos, freewill, wrestling with the Giant, his country, men of clay waltzing with bonfires shatter, a soldier's head at the Green Maiden, her sleepers dreaming a tower of fire, the Library burning to the ground with all their memories within, the fountain from which they drank, a stupor of deception under the sorceress' curse, the absinthe bars in the Wormwood Quarter where Calendria-Ellery lured her followers, redbreasts and Black Cats alike, unwittingly doing her bidding, Professor Ascalon the Rowan Knight sacrificing himself to wake his people from their nightmare.*

"Thelonious?"

His eyes snapped open. He could barely see Ellery standing outside the bars of his cell. She was dressed in her military uniform, her blood-red jacket lined with brown velvet. Gold medals on her lapel shone beside a row of brass buttons which led to her leather belt buckled about her waist with a fine sword at her side and high, black boots. Her stringy hair was pulled back into a severe soldier's knot under her feathered officer's hat. Thelonious chuckled miserably under his breath. They stared at each other for some time.

"Why'd you do it?" Thelonious rasped. "Why the Library?"

"Because it was another symbol. This time of the ruling class' superiority. Their last bastion of supposed wisdom and knowledge that grants them dominion over us. Now with no books to prove otherwise no man can say he is better equipped to rule than another. All men will be equal. All men will have nothing."

"You've just buried the uncertainty of our past in the depths of eternity," he said. "We will never know the truth about who we are or where we come from."

"That decision belongs to us," said Ellery. "It always has. Not to some musty pages." She was quiet for a moment. "You understand why it had to be you?"

Thelonious didn't seem to hear.

"You were an orphan, like me. You worked on Paradise Street, like me. You were raised by a man who taught you to care for the less fortunate. Everleague educated but still an outsider. I forged the professor's suicide note to name you the next secretary for the Bal Cypress Club. You had access to the Library, knowledge of how to concoct liquid fire from your studies. It was all there."

"You murdered the only person who ever loved me."

Ellery kicked at a rock with the toe of her boot.

"Why?" Thelonious's voice was a small, weak thing in the dark. "He believed in you. He would have helped you."

"He would have exposed me. Wanted to make public everything you know now. The plan wouldn't…"

"DAMN YOU AND YOUR PLAN!" Thelonious howled.

Ellery did not respond for the longest time. "They arrested my brother, Finn," she added, "He's to be executed for allowing you to escape. They think he's the informant in their ranks."

Thelonious laughed, a raking, coughing sound with tears in his eyes. "All your life you've tricked, betrayed and killed everyone close to you in pursuit of your goal. Is the price worth it? If you do live to see your new and better world, who will you share it with?"

"That doesn't matter anymore. Nothing matters except what we can change here, today. The free society we create will only be realized by those who come after us."

Thelonious spoke through clenched teeth. "I can only pray you suffer as much as you've caused others."

"I do," she said, easily as stating a fact. "I assure you, I do."

She pulled up a broken stool behind her and sat down. "But that's not why I'm here. You are to be executed tomorrow."

He giggled like a madman.

"You will be put on display so the Cabinet can announce they've finally caught the Paradise Street Dynamiter, leader of the Black Cats, and a grateful city will sleep soundly once again."

"Of course! What's one more drop of innocent blood on your hands?"

"I'm giving you a choice," she said. "Either stay in this cell and die tomorrow…or I'll let you go free tonight on the condition you take my place and become the Paradise Street Dynamiter."

Thelonious focused on her, incredulous.

"The word has gone out through my network of spies and assassins. They await your answer. If you agree they are ready to hide and protect you. They will be yours to command. Everything I've built, weapons stockpiles, safe houses, secret passages, even my recipe for liquid fire, all of it will be yours. Carry on what I've started. Continue to wage destruction against the rich and powerful and lead our people toward a new beginning."

"Your Evening King would allow this?"

"Hang the Evening King!" Ellery growled. "Who cares about the stupid, bloody Evening King anymore? *I'm* the Evening King! *You're* the Evening King! Don't you understand yet?"

"I don't trust you." Thelonious looked away, "If you let me go…I will try to kill you," he mused, more to himself than directed at her.

Ellery's eyes were also two dungeons. "I know," she said. "It'd be worth it."

He touched the cold chains on his hands.

"So? Have we a deal?"

Thelonious stared out his tiny, barred window at the first pale light of dawn on the horizon. The black smoke from the factories blotting out half the sky.

to be continued in
Part II: The Iron Servant

THE WIND IN MY HAIR IS MY CROWN

swift one of the woody glen
guide to thy warren of beast and men
dancer wild on the verdant hills
fleet-footed coney in wanton thrill
three hares entwine both moon and soul
I am rod to thy thicket nest in thy knoll
clover paw beneath the olive tree
our does our daughters lain with thee
dimpled dappled spring-shaded I
anointed with dew on thorny thigh
thy kingdom's pasture afar from towns
naked the wind in my hair is my crown
green desire bedded-bramble raised
let my mouth be ever wet with praise

Author Unknown

"What is a god?" I grimaced. I should have expected some half-assed attempt at the profound. He answered himself. "Power with personality." I was earning my interdisciplinary master's in religious studies at the time so I wasn't surprised when my friend Quaid, who teaches comparative mythology at the college, phoned with a major breakthrough. In his spare time Quaid was a leading researcher of Etruscan folklore. He knew I'd been reading Frazer's *The Golden Bough* when he called from Italy to say he'd discovered an obscure reference to a nature god that seemed to predate the Iron Age, Villanovan culture. "The name 'Tullus' or 'Tullum' was found on mosaics below Vatican City with an image of three rabbits connected by their ears. In the necropolis under St. Peter's Basilica, the foundations of what was once the Temple to Cybele, among the Egyptian obelisks and tombs of deceased Popes, this emblem is identical to one found beneath the Church of Mary Magdalene in France's Rennes-le-Château. The motif of three hares, a precursor to the

Celtic triquetra, is a common depiction of the 'triple deity' worshiped in various forms throughout pagan Europe (Maiden-Mother-Crone), Asia (Brahma-Vishnu Shiva) and the Christian Trinity. Tullus is described as a merry god of the forest. Any mention of him exists in a proto-Indo-European language of which we've only been able to partially interpret based on Etruscan cognates. The strange thing is, we have no idea who worshiped him. We assume an agro-pastoral society. Possibly the Picts once they migrated west from Scythia before the 1st Century, which connects Tullus to later Celtic 'green man' or sacred grove traditions. Except Tullus does not appear in any Italian pantheon. There are close equivalents: Sylvanus, Vertumnus and Faunus, for example. However, no Latin historian mentions him in their biographies of the region. Rabbits as fertility symbols made from bone or ivory are found throughout the Mediterranean in parts of Turkey, Algeria, Lebanon, Bulgaria, Morocco and Pakistan. The linguistic root of the name 'Tul' may be another loanword from any number of Afro-Asiatic languages meaning either 'earthenware' or 'to carry.' His exact culture of origin remains unclear but his mystery cult obviously once enjoyed a wide following. Tul reappears centuries later in the chivalric romances of the High Medieval period. A poem brought back from the Crusades, *Hymn to Tully*, recorded in the 1400s by Landaeus of Constantinople is a Christianized version of this same Tullus, reduced now from godhood to a harvest figure such as jack o' the green, the apple tree man, May king or John Barleycorn-type spirit of the grain field, which confirms that Tully found his way from the Near East to Gaul and the British Isles before the Romans where he'd already been adopted by the Druids." Quaid said he first read about Tully in the works of Landaeus of Constantinople found in the Vatican's archive (which, confidentially, he told me holds the largest collection of historical pornography). Landaeus was a Muslim-born bishop in the Byzantine Church from 1383 to 1462 who documented the art and practice of Balkan folk religions. Landaeus' monastic scripts contain the earliest version of the Tully poem, translated from Punic to Church Slavonic, as well as curious sketches of women dancing with rabbit-headed men. Landaeus comments that Tully's worship seems to predate any civilized society and evokes Neolithic superstition where distinction between human and animal is not clearly delineated, before the domestication of beasts when man shared equal kinship with the things he ate, as Tully is god of both. "ONCE IS NOTHING, TWICE IS CREATION, THE THIRD IS UNBEARABLE" wrote Landaeus. To this day no one is quite sure what this passage meant. A week after he returned from Italy Quaid said he'd almost finished translating a copy of *Hymn to Tully* into English and invited me to his house that evening to read the final product. On my drive over I thought about the significance of the number three: Pythagoras' triangle, past-present-future, Christ's temptations and days entombed, Peter's denials, comedy's rule, a sonata, Hermes "thrice-great" or Thoth "trismegistus", a genie's wishes, the lunar cycle, water's two hydrogen/one oxygen, the three act structure, *The Third Man*, the Three Secrets of Fátima, one, two, three, go! A lucky number like a rabbit's foot. Rabbits in various legends were believed to consort with witch-goddesses, warrior-queens and faeries including Artemis, Holda and Eostre (from where we get the word "Easter") as creatures connected to birth, spring and eternal recurrence. The "Man in the Moon" to Westerners would be the "Hare in the Moon" to people in China. Pliny the Elder recommended hare meat as a cure for sterility. Humorous Ojibwe tales are told about Nanabozho, a trickster cousin to Br'er Rabbit and Compère Lapin. The March Hare. Peter Cottontail. Bugs Bunny. I pulled up the driveway to Quaid's house to find the sliding screen door to his back porch left halfway open. A strong smell thick in the air as soon as I stepped out of my car. It wasn't altogether unpleasant so much as overpowering. I recognized this damp, earthy aroma from my childhood days in the country driving past richly tilled fields. As I climbed the steps to the porch I was astonished to find patches of grass and clover had overgrown the carpet like an indoor lawn, thick and dewy green. "Quaid?" I called out, risking a cautious step across the threshold. The living room had become, literally, a *living* room. Weeds and vines crept up the mantlepiece. Bees hummed from the vents. Sunlight streamed through cracks in the walls. What sounded like a waterfall trickled from the bathroom faucet. I gasped as I watched a dragonfly alight on what I realized was the body of a deer, her head and legs twisted among dandelion tufts, her ribs bare from where something fed on her remains. The couch, almost unrecognizable under a layer of moss, was covered in bird droppings and scads of molting fur.

I gazed up at an olive tree grown up through the coffee table, its roots ruptured the grassy floor beneath, its branches stooping down from the ceiling fan under the weight of its leafy drupes ripe for picking. And there was Quaid. What was left of him. He lay naked, the tree trunk growing up through his torso, splitting his body open into a hollow cavity like a dried gourd. Huddled in the gaping hole of his stomach lay three newborn rabbits. No snow-white, ruby-eyed, pointy-eared kits. They quivered in the nest of his entrails like pink, naked larva as his lifeless eyes stared upward, unblinking, into the green canopy.

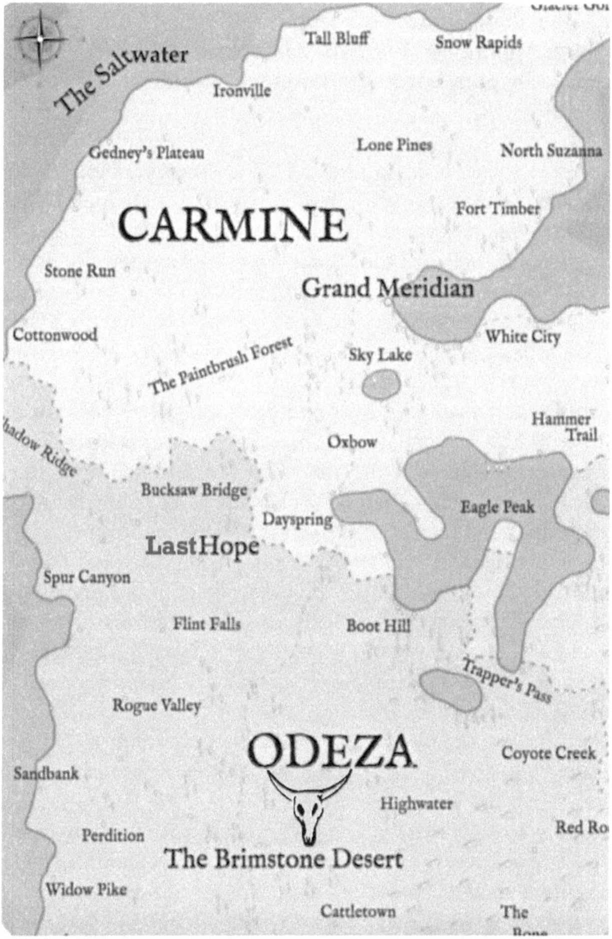

The Saltwater
Tall Bluff
Snow Rapids
Ironville
Gedney's Plateau
Lone Pines
North Suzanna
Fort Timber
CARMINE
Stone Run
Grand Meridian
Cottonwood
The Paintbrush Forest
Sky Lake
White City
Hammer Trail
Oxbow
Shadow Ridge
Bucksaw Bridge
Eagle Peak
Dayspring
LastHope
Spur Canyon
Flint Falls
Boot Hill
Trapper's Pass
Rogue Valley
ODEZA
Coyote Creek
Sandbank
Highwater
Perdition
The Brimstone Desert
Widow Pike
Cattletown
The

From the field notes of Deputy Marshal Bill Blaine, Lawfully Appointed Vigil of The Gold Pentacle, Grand Meridian Chapter, Sovereign Lodge of Carmine

-1-

New orders today. Ride to Odeza. Track down Eli Holt. Bring him to justice, dead or alive. I remember Eli. Gunfighter. Cattle rustler with the Sidewinder Gang. Lester Hickshaw's outfit, if memory serves. Many a moon since I last set foot in those parts. Holt ain't the most damnable piece of gallow-fodder I ever come across given what company he keeps. Him and Butch Canter, Big Al Rolland, Clarence Hopper, Pony Walsh. Aside from whiskey, women and cardhouse brawls Holt ain't much worse than the rest of them. All liver and lightning, those boys. Born with a buzzard's eye and a hankering for fire at breakfast. They can cuss up a whirlwind and ride their bobtail duns up a tree. But Holt has, to his detriment, taken up a vexating habit of shooting unarmed men. Plain, uncivilized murder. And not just any men. Day laborers who work for my uncle, Claypool Blaine, the railroad tycoon. I'm sent to find their killer, those poor boys who found the wrong end of Holt's revolver, not for the sake of their widows, but because their deaths was meant as a threat to the man what hired them. As I set pen to paper my uncle's company, United Steel, is laying track for the Grand Meridian Railway; the first freight line that will connect Carmine to Odeza. A mighty tall order. An undertaking of this magnitude is, of course, chock full of unpleasantness. Folks in the lowland don't take kindly to uplanders on the best occasions. Less so when they come hammering and shoveling through their homes saying it'll improve their purpose. It's hard country down there with more shallow graves than rocks to hide them. A feller raises himself or he don't get raised. You pound dirt into him, you're liable to find grit. Eli Holt ain't no exception. He's so bound and determined to stop them tearing up Odeza end to end he'll shoot any rail worker he claps eyes on. Duane Putnam, sheriff of Last Hope, organized a posse to go find Holt's hideout somewhere in the Brimstone Desert. Most of 'em never came back. It's gotten so ugly, Grand Marshal Willoughby Jessup warned me unless I bring in Holt by the end of this month either trussed up like a hog or counting worms in a pine box, he'll have my badge. I've given half my life to become a marshal. I ain't about to let a bad-bellied coward like Holt ruin me. If he don't stink of death I never saw a carcass. It'll sorrow me some to pull the trigger. I used to run with that wild bunch of his before I turned lawman. But Holt made his choice long ago and so did I. As a sworn vigil of the Gold Pentacle I'm honor-bound to uphold the code of the Almanac. Backshooters have no place in right society whatever their motives. You can't go killing a man just because you don't truck with his profession. Grand Marshal Jessup also has ties to the railroad. He and Claypool Blaine must have some under-the-table deal. I don't know the first thing about politics but I reckon Jessup's rise through the ranks of Carmine's Sovereign Lodge had a lot to do with Blaine and his golden handshake. Buying votes. Winning the people. Blaine's support might lead to Jessup becoming the new Elect in Carmine. That's why Jessup is so gung-ho on catching Holt. To keep Blaine happy and his steel track on progress. It's a two day ride to Last Hope. Nothing good comes from that place.

-2-

Arrived in Last Hope on Hoburn's Day so the general store was closed. Whole town out dancing in the street. Rented a room above Diamondback Saloon. Mayor of Last Hope, Douglass T. Gedney, still an old, sore-sided boar. Crooked as barrel of snakes. He met me at the bar and offered me a drink on the house. "We're dry and whiskey's wet," he said by way of a toast. I told him I don't partake while on the job. He don't much cherish the notion of a Gold Pentacle marshal sniffing around his town. He has a fine line to tread. On the one hand it don't behoove him to let an outsider go eyeballing his affairs too closely; the gambling and whoring what goes on in his establishment. On the other hand, he knows I'm here to put down the man who's slowing the railroad. A train station in Last Hope would mean more big city money pouring into his little town. As today was a holiday ladies wore tana blossoms in their hair while men drank and sang songs. I heard one we used to sing when I was a boy:

Child, go riding on the road tonight,
wild and wicked with nothing to hide,
you don't know yet but will by and by - no-how.

They can take my money, they can take my fame, don't care none, it always stays the same,
I don't need nothing not even my name - no one.

Stars lie dotted on the southbound land, go and gather them in your hand, oh no, dust and dreams! Hey, hey, hey, dust and dreams for me!

Child, beware of that ol' black mare,
she takes more than any man can bear,
done gave up everything to go wayfare - nowhere.

When I'm looking at a city so grand,
all this talking I don't understand,
ain't nothing lost like the heart of man - always.

Moonlight shining on the sundown land, go and watch it slip from your hand, oh no, dust and dreams! Hey, hey, hey, dust and dreams for me!

Tell your mama she can say goodbye,
the day you're born is the day you die,
I know it's not right but I don't cry - no ma'am.

Boys and girls played on toy drums and fifes and wore paper masks of vultures, bulls, lizards and other faces from the story. A little girl offered me a traditional cup of *ascazuma*, a drink the Kahotey used to make from bitter cocoa and fire peppers. Hoburn's Day festivities include barn dances, parades and firecrackers to commemorate the proud saga of Red Hoburn who discovered Odeza long ago. He felled mountaintops, rode storms, skinned moondoggies and other such flap-jaw. Over the years as the first settlers made contact with the Kahotey tribes cowboys told stories of ol' Red Hoburn around their campfires, each more outlandish and highfalutin with the telling. They call him the "Land-Tamer" and believe he's the great-great-granddaddy of all us lowlanders. I grew up in Odeza so I'd like to think I better understand their ways but most anyone with book-learning up Grand Meridian way don't reckon he ever drew breath at all.

-3-

Why the railroad is so acquisitive of a law-forsaken wasteland like Odeza is beyond me! It's a blood-stew of feuding criminals. The Brimstone Desert covers everything. Ain't nothing but duststorms, tar pits and quicksand. All that grows here is fever grass, ghost sage, touch-me-not and widow's-bane or some poisonous mushroom at night. Then there are all manner of diseases: yellow vein, sweet rash, sun pox. Talked to the town drunk, Doc Remedy; huckster, fat man in a top hat who runs a traveling chuckwagon. Sells bottles of "miracle tonic" supposed to cure these and every known ailment. Nothing lives out in the Brimstone except walking snakes, flying rats and who knows what else. I've seen swarms of flesh-eating gutflies that can strip a horse to bone in under an hour. There are cactus cats, hair sharp as razors, that breed in patches of tana cactus. Its orange blossoms were sacred to the Kahotey people who once lived here. Tana juice gave their medicine men visions to speak the "dreamtalk" but cooked wrong it can make a man crazy. Like them roaming smoke mystics, "Coldbloods" they call themselves. Coldbloods may be the most popular religion in Odeza but also the least understood. They practice, more or less, the rituals leftover by the Kahotey that settlers adopted. Though you'd be hard pressed to find more than a passing resemblance between that old wildcraft and what it's become. The Kahotey worshiped water, rocks, the sun and wind. Now folks observe the faith in their own ways. Some eat the tana cactus and sit in a sweat lodge to see visions. Others go on pilgrimage into the desert where they walk for days without food or water. But most simply wear a rattlesnake tail as a necklace or horny toad teeth as earrings or an iguana claw as a ring. Little tokens of favor. They have no leaders to speak of except a few wisefolk like that smoke woman in her tent by the crossroads on the outskirts of town. "Ma Weena" we used to call her. She claims she knows the old Kahotey rootwork and smoke-tricks but she'll say anything to fill her pockets. She's been dabbling in bad medicine since before rain was wet. I remember a man went to her to join the Coldbloods. They found him days later wandering out of the desert, covered in boils from sun pox, screaming about a monster sleeping beneath the burning sand. Her tana juice drove him loony as a crosseyed hound! When I was young my best friends, Lev and Wilkie Calico, couldn't stop eating the cactus.

They kept little tana buds in their pockets to chaw on. Turned their teeth orange. They thought it was a laugh, gawking at stupefying sights that wasn't there. Desert madness. A man's senses betray him if he lingers too long in the Brimstone. It's an evil place. And if you go out there with anger in your belly or lust and greed in your heart it rings the dinner bell for all manner of dark things to come running, grinning, breathing their breath on you. The Kahotey had a word for such evil. I won't try to spell it here, but the gist of it meant "iron death."

-4-

Wanted posters for Eli Holt in every window, on every door. Up to 1,000 gold bits. Claypool Blaine's reach is as wide as his pockets are deep.

-5-

Odeza's changed since I been away. Today I came to a white clapboard church. Went inside to find folks dressed in in black, holding candles on wooden pews. At the front of the church above the pulpit was a painting of a giant scorpion. The preacher man gave me a dirty look all the way in the back row. I asked Mayor Gedney what that place was. He told me it's the First Chapel of the Dawn Raiser. They pray to Ikthil'i, that giant scorpion. They call it their savior because it "visits its wrath upon sinners." In other words, it eats anyone they don't approve of. All my life I ain't heard nothing charitable about them ugly sand-bugs regardless of size, so the notion of praying to the king-bitch stud of 'em all seems a might foolhardy. My uncle was bit by a scorpion once. His leg swelled up big and red as a side of hickory beef. Would've finished him had my aunt not known how to suck the poison out. Ikthil'i is said to live somewhere in Spur Canyon but it's also been seen prowling the hills and valleys in the surrounding area hunting for stray cattle and the like. Few who've clapped eyes on this monster lived to tell of it. It leaves a sticky venom on the ground where it crawls. Anyone who touches it comes down with a nasty case of yellow vein; sores and blisters on their skin oozing puss before paralysis sets in. The church sees this as punishment for wrongdoing. "No man can escape his sting," they say. The congregation takes a vow of purity, even in marriage outside childbearing, no drinking, dancing, colorful clothing, singing, cards or dice. Cave paintings found in the Shadow Ridge Mines near Last Hope picture scorpions with women in their pinchers, laying eggs in men, devouring children in their sleep. No one knows for sure who painted them. I figure the Kahotey. Lot of powerful unfriendly varmints in the desert. Perhaps the Kahotey drew them pictures on the walls by way of warning but settlers came along and misread it as religion. I'll tell you one thing, from what little Kahotey I've picked up over the years, the word "Ikthil'i" sure as hell don't mean "Dawn Raiser." The preacher man, Reverend Drexel Barnhart, says according to the old paintings Ikthil'i leaves its nest each morning to seek out the wicked and strike judgment on them. Seems Odeza's become a place of even more consternation and worriment than when I left.

-6-

Saw a ghost today. Lev Calico. Leaning against a mesquite tree. The spitting image of his old self. I didn't recognize him until he pulled his bandana off that sly grin of his. I shook my head. Thought it was a heat mirage. When I looked again he was gone. Ain't possible. Lev Calico is dead. I should know. I buried him in the Brimstone Desert five years ago. Before I moved north to Grand Meridian and became a deputy marshal I was an outlaw with the Calico Brothers, the roughest riders in Odeza. Lev, Wilkie and me were like family since we was greenhorn kids in our hometown of Lantana, known to hoop and holler and bend an elbow at a bar each night. Lev recruited only the most dash-fire young bucks to help them rustle cattle and hold up stagecoaches. I was with them, saddle to saddle, for years. A wanted man. 300 silver bits on my head. We robbed a bank in Bucksaw. We raided the goldmine in Perdition. We ended the whiskey wars between the Lucky Seven and the Red Hand Gang, both our rivals, and took over Thunderhead Range ourselves. We were the most feared bandits Odeza had ever seen. I'd be with them to this day, still sinning and shooting, had I not found Lev burying my wife's body in a cactus patch. Lev was slobbering drunk, "He's coming!" Lev screamed, "He's coming! I didn't mean to, Billy! He made me! He made me! He woulda done worse to her! He'll destroy us all when he comes!" "Who?" I asked. "Iron death," he said, "Sleeping fire. All dust and dreams now. All dust and dreams." I saw the mad gleam in his eye and the orange froth at his mouth from the tana buds. My wife's blood was still running down his hands. I emptied six bullets into his head. Then I went after Wilkie. I didn't stop until I tracked down and killed every member of my old gang. Sick with anger and grief I cut dirt all the way north to Carmine to start a new life. Got arrested soon as I set foot in Grand Meridian. Willoughby Jessup was good enough to spare me. "Billy Blaine," he said, "I've heard of you. Seems I owe you my thanks. We been after the Calico Brothers for nigh on more years than I got fingers to count. You put 'em under in one day. Seems to me you're more on our side than theirs." Instead of jail and the rope he offered to train me as his deputy marshal. "Black days ahead," he said, "Civilization's coming for Odeza whether it likes it or not. Bound to be trouble and I aim to come out on top. I'll need someone who knows the terrain down there. Someone who understands the outlaw mind." I'm forever beholding to Jessup for setting me straight. It was before I found the Almanac and learned its code of honor. I've been working out my redemption ever since, brining badmen to justice and keeping the peace in these troublesome parts.

-7-

Asking questions about Eli Holt in this town's a surefire way to get you a heap a' nothing. Odezans are suspicious of strangers, especially a lawman who was once a horse thief. They still remember me as the young cutthroat who double-crossed the Calico Brothers and murdered his partners for a gold badge. I'd get more answers from a stone. I rode out to Rogue Valley that used to be our hideout. Figured Eli might have gone there. No sign of him.

-8-

I'm not the only one on Eli's trail. A bounty hunter named "Warlock" came through the general store to buy a pound of hardtack. Odd fella. No horse. Travels on foot. Wide-brimmed hat. Little brown pouch around his neck. Fringed buckskins and dusty leathers. Knives in his belt. Wears a painted wool blanket over one shoulder like the Kahotey. Patchy beard almost covering scars on his cheeks. Told me he wasn't after Eli for the reward. Says he's on a quest to hunt the deadliest gunmen Odeza has to offer. Thinks he becomes stronger with every kill he makes. Been working his way up from wrestling cactus cats to fighting every bushwhacker in the territory. Probably a Coldblood by the looks of him. Talks like one anyhow. Says every day he drinks a drop of viper blood every day that he keeps in a jar in his pouch to build up immunity. Pray I'll never cross his path again.

-9-

Last night, after most the town bedded down, I saw a group of boys haul a man by his shirt into the saloon. I followed. Rowdy drunks with itchy triggers. The man they were rough-handling was a Kahotey. An elderly one with gray skin. They dragged him to the bar, held his arms to his sides and forced a glass of whiskey down his gullet. These boys were laughing and jeering, calling the old man names. The old man, he don't say more than blink. He just stands put without struggle. These boys kept choking the old man on firewater. Beating a dead mule don't make a fight of it, so I stepped in. "Leave him be and it won't come to irons." The boys howled and whistled at me, feeling their oats. "Don't you get the carry of this, son?" I asked. One of them slapped leather. I shot him where he stood before he could tickle his hilt. The rest scattered. I helped the old man back to his tent on the outskirts of town.

The Almanac:
Book of Independence
Article 5th, Section H

Hoburn, Red: A character invented by the Sovereign Lodge of Carmine. Humorous tales written about a tall, sullen, formidable gunfighter to popularize southward expansion into the Odezan territory that have since taken on an oral tradition of their own. Impossible tales such as Hoburn was raised by coyotes on the Pale Plains or "once got into a fistfight with a thunderstorm and licked it so bad rain ain't never dared come back to Odeza since!" The stories all agree he was found by the Kahotey, the nature-worshiping natives who once inhabited Odeza and later became a trail guide and treaty-maker for the first wagoners in their early contact with the natives. Some have him wielding a legendary revolver known as "Durnwin the Black Mare"; a weapon said to kill anyone unworthy who tried to fire it. The name "Kahotey" means, in their language, "People of the Sun." Settlers called them "manyskins" after their ability to change colors like a lizard to blend in with their desert surroundings. Most Kahotey were rust red, sandy orange and ash gray. A diminutive race, never more than five feet in height, they were slender with six long fingers on each hand, hairless bodies, smooth, round faces with no nose or ears and very large, almond-shaped eyes the color of deep amber. When Hoburn first encountered the Kahotey they didn't know what to make of him. They thought he was a dumb, lumbering giant. They were puzzled by his black hair and blue eyes. Hoburn befriended their Chief River-Path who named him "Land-Tamer" and taught him a secret ritual using tana cactus called *ixlaan* or "dreamtalk", which they believed enabled them to speak with the dead. From the Hoburn tales we obtained supposed translations of many Kahotey words including *wachicoatl* meaning "wayworker" or "man of knowledge", and *tupatec*, their word for settlers, meaning "infant-giant." The tales claim the Kahotey could levitate their bodies off the ground and possessed the power to raise storms at will. There are one or two documented incidents where a Kahotey warrior was being chased by a rancher when a sudden downpour covered his escape, a fierce wind destroyed an unwelcome campsite or a lightning bolt struck a prospector trespassing on their land. After this Untamed Age our Founders handed down to us the righteous code of the Almanac. The Gold Pentacle was founded in Grand Meridian, its Appointed Vigils ordained by the Sovereign Lodge of Carmine as a brotherhood of marshals dedicated to protect us.

Letter from Ma Weena to Miss Velveteen c/o the Diamondback Saloon

Dear Sister,

I hope this letter finds you well. No doubt you've heard Raven's-Dance was late in the town last night when he got jumped at your place by Bo Gedney and his flunkies. They would've drowned him in whiskey, the stupid pigs, if that uplander deputy hadn't broken them up. He fixed Bo with one bullet then brought Raven's-Dance home to me. No sooner had the deputy left our tent with nothing but our thanks, shots rang out from the dark that dropped him cold. No telling who's to blame. Honest men are scarce as water these days. Could've been anyone. Might be this Eli Holt, the one that ranger was sent to collect. Could've been one of them hot-mouthed colts from the saloon looking to settle the score. There'll be hell to pay for killing the mayor's boy. Raven's-Dance and I buried the deputy up in the hills. Got rid of any trace of him. Carmine will be spitting nails. They been anxious for any excuse to move on us, always looking down their barrel, waiting till they had a good enough reason in their sights. Now they've got one. If they find the deputy's body they'll send enough law-dogs to overrun our town, flashing their fancy yellow stars, making us obey that little black book of theirs. It'll mean the end for Odeza. I have a knowing about this. Strange rumbles brewing. Crying in the wind. The wells are drying up. The railroad cutting up our land, bringing more outsiders. The steer are dying and no one can say why. Remember we once saw a cow with sweet rash? She strayed too far and got into a patch of touch-me-not. She kept scratching and scratching against a fencepost until she bled, trying to rip her own skin off from the pain. Pa had to put her down. It's no itchweed making the herds sick. It's something worse. No sign or mark on them. They just keel over. People say the Calico Brothers are alive again. Little Ida Mae said she saw Lev and Wilkie stagger past her window one night, moonlight shining through the holes in their heads. She's not one for telling tales. After we buried the deputy, Raven's-Dance had another of his shaking spells. He saw a vision of a longhorn skull crossing the Pale Plains which spoke to him. I wrote down his words:

"Thunder drums. Dark clouds on the horizon. Iron death walks above. Sleeping fire awakens below. Three dead men ride a black mare to the golden ruin. Then only dust and dreams."

When he came to his senses I asked what it meant. He couldn't answer. What do you think? When he has these fits he says he can see what he calls the "great web" of mysteries the world was built on that binds all living things, mountains, sky, animals, people, everything together. Learning at the feet of the last Kahotey wayworker has taught me much: how to brew tana blossom for the dreamtalk, although I must confess, I've not yet gained any predictions. Perhaps it doesn't work the same on our kind. It's driven many a good man clean out of his head. Raven's-Dance told me when growing cactus flower one must always remember the green wisdom of plants is a language same as any tongue of men. The tana wishes to be heard, to tell us its stories; stories of things below the earth: roots, gold, bones. Everything Raven's-Dance taught me I wrote down. After his partner, Forgotten-Rains, died a few years ago he said it was a comfort to have someone to share his final years with. Something's coming, Velvet. A war. A storm. Raven's-Dance says there's evil beneath Odeza. Something long dormant just beginning to stir. The noise of the railroad has disturbed it and once it awakens to the world above nothing can stop it. Red Horburn woke it once. Unlike all the yarns about our benevolent Land-Tamer, Hoburn was sent to wipe out the Kahotey to pave the way for settlers to steal their land. Hoburn and his riders dumped so many bodies in the Brimstone Desert they turned Odeza into a mass grave. Something deep down inside our land woke for the first time. Pray it don't rise again. Burn this letter after you read it. May the gentler spirits keep you.

Love, Weena

Ace Telegraph Co.
Incorporated Cable Service

From: Mr. Claypool Blaine, United Steel Headquarters, Grand Meridian, Carmine

To: Grand Marshal Willoughby Jessup, Last Hope, Odeza

No word from your deputy • Missing five days • Mayor's son murdered • Holt still at large • More railroad shootings • Judge Haggin to reconvene Citizen's Committee • vote in one week • Find Holt or another job

Field notes of Willoughby Jessup, Grand Marshal of The Gold Pentacle, Sovereign Lodge of Carmine

-322-

I hate Odeza. Hot, miserable, half-dead place. It's a backwards people what live here. When they're not drinking themselves stupid or shooting each other in the back they're up to their necks in hokum. The ones that don't go around playing dress-up in snakeskin think God is a sting-beetle the size of a barn. Tarnation, that's damn near intolerable! Sent two of my best men, Cass Harris and Vernon Mercer, ahead of me looking for Bill Blaine, that sorry fool. Never saw hide nor hair of him again. Last I heard, Billy carried a Kahotey elder into the Pale Plains; that stretch of desert just outside Last Hope where the sands run white as salt. Harris came back struck blind in both eyes after his pony trod on some fever grass. The scent will do that to a man. Stings your nose and waters your eyes until your sight goes all bleary-like. If not treated in time the lights fade out for good. He'll never be no use in the saddle again. Still, Harris was the lucky one. Vern got mauled by a pack of cactus cats. Tore his arms and legs clean off. Hardly anything left of him. Hateful place, Odeza. Everything here'll try to kill you. More trouble than it's worth. Claypool's masterplan -for Carmine to annex Odeza into one, big Freestate- will mean war. Lowlanders ain't gonna sit quiet while we slip the bridle in their mouth. Must be why Holt's killing so many people to stop the railroad from coming. Sooner I find Bill and get out, the better.

-323-

Found the corpse of a young Kahotey woman. A chief 's daughter, most like, what with the necklace of colorful beads she wore. The smell! I found her lying in the blinding sand, bright as pure snow, behind a black rock. She'd been ripening in the sun a long time. Two, three days, if I'd hazard a guess. Flesh browning and crispy, rotting off the bone. Surprised buzzards or gutflies hadn't got to her. She wasn't shot and there weren't no signs of anything gnawing her. I thought the Kahotey avoided this area because they couldn't blend into the white sand. For all their tricks, knowing how to change colors, the Pale Plains was the one place those manyskins couldn't sneak around and hide. It's why early homesteaders built Last Hope here, surrounded for a mile in every direction by pearly-white dunes where the savages was less like to risk bothering them. There was something else too. What was it? Moondoggies, that's it. This is where moondoggies are said to roam at night. 'Course nobody puts much stock in them campfire yarns. Why a Kahotey girl wandered onto this taboo ground when she knew she weren't safe don't make a lick of sense.

-324-
Ambush! Kahotey girl not dead. Decoy. Some kind of mirage. Attacked by Kahotey hunting party. Ten, fifteen warriors. Couldn't see where I was shooting. Fires without heat. Blood pouring from the rocks. Wind whipping up dust devils. Sun went black at midday. The desert suddenly covered in corpses of men, women and children. Kahotey smoke-tricks. Out of bullets. I hear them now. Close.

A page from "Dust & Dreams: Ma Weena's Cookbook, Odezan Folklore, Sayings of Raven's Dance"

Ballad of Red Hoburn

Take the rope around my neck,
up upon the railroad track.
Fiery winds are at my back,
painted spirits attack.
I'm looking out but cannot see
the hangman's daughter all in black,
staring at me like a fool.
Her stolen heart, secret jewel.

As the waters start to rise
my lack of fear is no surprise.
Save me from God, don't let me die,
no grave could bury all my lies.
The desert smoke, a sacrifice.
From the bridge watch amber eyes.

Underneath a pale gray sky,
as these shadows pass me by
of my life I wasted when
I bought and sold my fellow men.
They pull the shroud over my gaze
and first thing's last, I stand amazed.
Has faith alone been of no use?
My prayer has become the noose.

JOHNNY WHITMAN,

American Dragonslayer

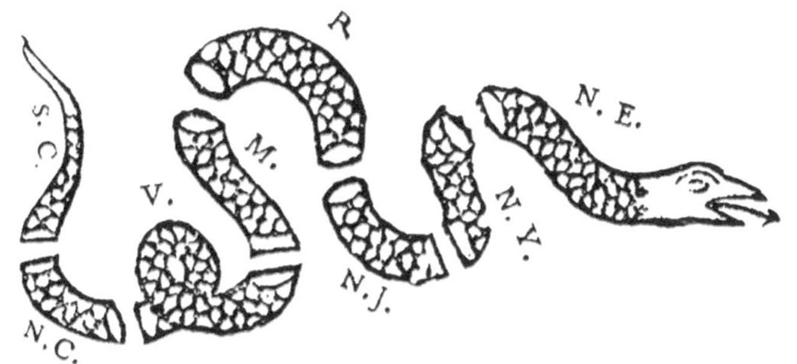

1789

It was known as a "Roanoke red." He could tell by its bright, crimson scales and the black pattern around its eyes and throat. Four wings like that of a monstrous cardinal furled around its hind legs. The dragon was about twenty feet long from nose to tail. Not especially large as far as dragons go. Downy, red feathers stuck out between hard, overlapping plates along its sides. Its slender, barbed tail thrashed wildly in the creek, churning the shallows into rapids near a creaking waterwheel as its neck darted in and out of a hole it had dug near the mill. It crunched a wooden barrel of apple mash in its powerful, beaklike jaws, gulping down fermented juices by the gallon. Twenty miles south of Boston tucked away on a quiet bend of the Indian Head River, Godly Wood, Massachusetts was a sleepy farm town in the remote, New England forest sheltered by elm and walnut trees. Van Brummell's Cider Mill, renowned for their apple brandy harvested every year from the nearby Hesper Orchards was the only major industry in this part of the countryside. Now their rosy-gold bushels were scattered in the rushes as the dragon tore through the buried cellar, biting stored casks in half to guzzle the autumn liquor. Fourteen-year-old Johnny Whitman watched the rampant, feathered lizard destroy the mill with mild fascination. He'd never seen a dragon this close before. "It's a full-grown 'drake'," he thought, remembering the proper term for a male dragon of mating age. "Not all of them breathe fire," he reminded himself. "But isn't their blood venomous?" He tried to recall a book he'd read by Cotton Mather. In Mather's sermons on Salem witchcraft the Puritan minister wrote that dragons are the oldest foe of man, offspring of the Devil and enemies of Christendom, therefore vulnerable to prayers or any verse of scripture. However, the Iroquois believed that the *Oniare* or Horned Serpents came from beyond the northern sky on a land bridge before the sun was born. Their ancestral tribes hunted dragons nearly to extinction as they had the woolly mammoth and sabretooth tiger long ago. Dragon-hide was as valuable to the natives for stronger-than-leather clothing material as it was to later French fur trappers; rarer than beaver pelts and worth more than caribou skin. This particular breed was named the "Roanoke red" after the Lost Colony due to the gruesome part its kind played in the settlers' disappearance. English colonists first encountered New World dragons in the Year of Our Lord 1590. Sir Walter Raleigh heard rumor of great worms on the continent when he charted his maiden voyage across the Atlantic. Such beasts had been more or less subdued throughout Europe between Hadrian's Wall and the dawn of the Enlightenment. The rise of Catholicism during the Middle Ages led to the decline of dragons at the hands of holy warriors from Beowulf to Saint George. Raleigh, a vain opportunist eager to establish his own overseas outpost for Queen Elizabeth I, decided it was worth the risk. A hundred and fifteen families at Roanoke had been burned alive or eaten in one night. A grim reminder that the British Empire's first step to tame this vast and unexplored frontier could not be taken lightly. Johnny stood on the opposite bank watching broken, wooden barrels float downstream. "Shame to waste all that cider," he thought. The youngest of ten brothers, Johnny was considered the least among his family. Small in stature, a bit of a daydreamer and a layabout Johnny wasn't much of a soldier and even less of a field-hand. The Whitmans owned a modest acreage in Godly Wood since his grandfather, Jehoshaphat Whitman, retired from the tea and tobacco trade in Jamestown after sailing with the East India Company. Most of Johnny's brothers had been killed in the Revolutionary War. The ones that survived either went overseas or worked the farm when their father came down with spotted fever. The future of the Whitman's farm was a debatable prospect. Without enough labor in the face of mounting debts, Johnny was forced to pull twice his weight to provide for his family. Which is how he happened upon the cider mill that day in his donkey-drawn wagon on his way to sell bags of horse feed in Boston. He heard what, at first, sounded like a bear, but bigger and louder than any bear he'd ever heard. His donkey whickered nervously as it stamped the ground. As Johnny watched the drake gorge itself on cider he suddenly felt angry. It wasn't fair, this winged monster drinking the Van Brummells out of business. They'd been brewers in Godly Wood for generations. Someone ought to teach that creature some manners. Without thinking he scooped up a pebble from the creek and flung it at the dragon's head. The beast roared and shook itself as the stone connected with a bony spike. Whipping its neck around, jowls dripping with fruit pulp, the dragon spotted him across the water.

"You there, boy!" the dragon hissed. "What is the meaning of this?"

"It's a game," said Johnny.

The dragon tapped its massive talons on the ground. "Do I strike you as the friendliest playmate?" it asked.

"Here are the rules," Johnny continued. "If I can hit you between the horns you'll share one barrel of cider with me."

"I prefer a simpler game," the dragon growled. "It has one rule: I leap across this brook and devour the stupid little boy who throws rocks at me."

"Are you a bird?" asked Johnny.

The dragon snorted indignantly. "Have you no eyes, fool?" It spread its four, red wings for emphasis. "Could the mightiest oak support my nest?" it bellowed. It took a step toward him down the grassy slope. Its front legs buckled underneath its mass, stumbling to one side before it caught its balance. In that brief misstep Johnny realized something. One detail that tipped the scales in his favor. The dragon was drunk.

"You shouldn't be in there," Johnny scolded. "This is the Van Brummells' mill. It's their cider you're stealing."

The dragon snarled deep in its throat. "I lived here before this mill was built. When these apple trees were still seedlings. Before you or any Two-Legs set foot on this land. These orchards are mine! The soil, the water, mine! If a man breaks into *my* house and raids *my* larder and cooks a meal on *my* hearth, can he sit down to *my* table and claim it is *his* supper?"

Johnny reached for a length of rope in the back of his wagon. "All the same, you're being quite rude. You should fly away, bird."

The dragon snapped its fanged beak. "I wonder if your bravery will improve your flavor?"

With a roar it charged into the creek. Lumbering downhill into the sluggish current the drunken reptile swayed, unable to advance in a straight line. Johnny lassoed his rope around the dragon's head. Tugging with all his strength, Johnny threw the other end into the mill's waterwheel. The rope tightened around the dragon's neck as it twisted in the spinning paddles. Smoke rose from the dragon's nostrils. A spurt of flame was cut short. The knot constricted its windpipe. Now up to its belly in the water the dragon howled and thrashed in a frenzy of foam and mud, straining against the noose's stranglehold. Its wings flapped then folded like paper fans. A hideous gurgling escaped from its open maw as its forked tongue flailed helplessly. Another minute of struggle, another lurch, another shudder and its lifeless bulk sank to the creek bottom. He'd done it. He'd killed a dragon. Then he noticed something glimmering among the reeds at the edge of the water. Bending over to inspect it he found a gold guinea sticking out of the mud. With its last breath the dragon had spat out the coin. Johnny then remembered stories of dragons hoarding treasure. Where there was one piece, there had to be more. As he stood there thinking, he heard a scuffle behind a nearby tree. Turning, he saw an elderly man in tan breeches and tricorne hat, carrying a musket. Johnny recognized him. "You're Old Man Van Brummell," he said.

"That I am. Who might you be?"

"John Whitman's youngest son. My father bought a cask of brandy from you last spring."

"Ah yes." He looked at the dragon's half-submerged body.

"But…don't tell me you did this?"

Johnny smiled proudly and folded his arms. "Indeed I did."

Van Brummell pointed with a trembling finger. "Ol' Mandoag terrorized these parts for years."

"Mandoag?"

"That's his name. Though folks around here called him the 'Firebird.' How'd you do it? I fired my blunderbuss at him but the buckshot just ricocheted off his scales."

"I hung him."

The old man laughed until he coughed. "You must be a courageous young man to slay a full-grown drake. Hardly anyone I ever heard of has done it and lived." There were few American dragons left. They were defeated by famous heroes like Alfred "Old Stormalong" Bulltop, Molly Pitcher, Passaconaway, even the Sons of Liberty hunted one or two in their time. "They say General Washington killed an albino dragon near the Delaware. During the winter of Valley Forge, if memory serves. Named it 'White Vortigern.' He mounted its head at Mount Vernon. I seen his portrait. Him with one boot resting on its skull, big as a carriage. Proud day for us all."

Johnny heard the story before but wasn't sure if he believed it. Like every Yankee he knew a white dragon symbolized Anglo-Saxons, King George and centuries of English tyranny. It stood to reason that Washington, soon to become their first president, concocted this tall tale as a bit of patriotic theater. He suspected

Washington found the white dragon already dead in the snow when he took its head as a trophy.

"I owe you my thanks, son," Van Brummell chortled. "I wish there was some way I could repay you but, as you can see, my whole life was in that mill and now it's in shambles."

Johnny turned the gold coin over in his hand. "Do you have a knife?" he asked. He waited as Van Brummell hurried inside what was left of the mill and returned with a cavalry saber.

"I took this off a Hessian rider during the war," said Van Brummell proudly. Johnny hefted the weighty blade onto his shoulder and waded into the creek.

"What are you doing?" Van Brummell demanded. Johnny was up to his waist in the freezing water before he reached Mandoag's corpse. With both hands he raised the sword above his head and plunged it into the dragon's underbelly. Black blood and steam poured from the wound like burning mercury. The water boiled on contact. A noxious stench overpowered his lungs. Johnny leapt back and splashed ashore before the dark, bubbling pool could reach him.

"The sword!" Van Brummell gasped. "Look at the sword!"

Johnny looked down at the hilt in his hand. Half of the blade had melted away. The heat of the dragon's innards was enough to dissolve solid steel.

"Whatever possessed you to do that?" Van Brummell asked.

Johnny held up the golden coin. "I thought it might have swallowed the rest for safekeeping."

Van Brummell laughed. "Why, don't you know nothing about dragons? Their stomachs is so full of sulfur that ain't nothing goes in ever comes out again. Besides…" he took a confidential step closer. "…they say he keeps his gold in a hollow tree somewhere in the middle of the orchard. Captain Kidd's treasure, most like. But nobody's ever found it. Not that anyone's dared to look."

Leaving his wagon, donkey and grain behind, Johnny set off into the apple trees.

"Where you going?" Van Brummell called after him.

After hiking a few miles through the orchards Johnny came to a clearing where the leaves and bark on all the surrounding branches had been scorched black. None of the fruit had ever grown back. One gnarled, dead tree looked particularly blighted. Next to its roots Johnny found a skeleton dressed in a Redcoat's uniform. He grinned. This must be the place. Using the metal stump of his sword to hack away at the hollow trunk he soon broke through the charred, rotten wood. Nestled inside was a rusty chest with a British naval insignia on the lid. The *HMS New Troy* sent from Oak Island, addressed to General Cornwallis. Throwing aside the broken padlock Johnny found the chest was full of hundreds of gold guineas. The cargo from some warship, no doubt. Funds sent to finance their soldiers. But the final Battle of Yorktown ended eight years ago. All the men who'd fought to defend this treasure were dead now. Johnny couldn't believe his fortune. He was a hero. He had a box full of riches. Nothing stood in his way to become a respectable gentleman. He would take a handful of coins back to Van Brummell. A little something for him to repair the damages. Another pile he would send home to the farm. He could just picture the astonished resentment on his brothers' faces. The rest he'd keep. Providence had smiled on him. He would not waste his second chance at a new beginning. Word would spread. He would reinvent himself. Start a new life and a new profession as a dragonslayer.

Traveling south through the pines down the King's Highway toward Charleston Johnny was exhausted and night was falling. He was on his way to Savannah, Georgia to investigate reports of a carnivorous vine in the bayou. Over the last year he had been hired to drive out a banshee from a lighthouse in Elizabethtown, Maryland. Before that he'd been called on to kill a Stonecoat, an Iroquois giant, that stole and cooked ponies from a ranch in Vermont. Then there was the black dog that attacked lumberjacks in Rhode Island, the witch who cast diseases on children in New Hampshire and the hairy man sighted near Popham on the Canadian border. For someone who'd built his reputation on dragonslaying, he'd encountered only one dragon on his adventures throughout New England. There was that water-panther in the Hudson; a *mishipeshu*, half-fish, half-cougar, that kept overturning ferryboats and eating the passengers along with their livestock. He scouted the along the riverbank until he found the gill-cat's underwater grotto at a small fork where he built a dam, draining its lair, leaving it to writhe–webbed paws scratching, tail fins slapping–

and dry out in the sun. He'd made a fine dragon-hide coat out of Mandoag, purchased brown leather boots with brass buckles, a walking stick, knapsack and tin canteen. Despite his notoriety, being publicly lauded as "vanquisher of fearsome critters" by none other than Daniel Boone, Johnny knew that he'd survived this past year on luck, lies and trickery. The banshee in the lighthouse, which old folks claimed was a *tah-tah-kle-ah*, turned out to be just a screech owl roosting under the eaves. He cleared out its nest but still accepted payment for sending the evil spirit back to the grave. There were other misunderstandings he'd taken advantage of. The stone giant was still a child; three times the size of a normal man but average height for its race at that age. Johnny had frightened away the young giant by setting off a powder keg near its head while it slept. The black dog wasn't a hellhound, just a wolf with hydrophobia. And the witch was just an old woman making folk medicine for sick children in her village. As for the hairy man, a *chenoo*, or ice cannibal from the north, Johnny never saw him but he skinned a possum's hide which he brought back as the brute's scalp. He made his living as a fraud. There had been one or two other near brushes with death but he knew, deep down, it was only a matter of time before people discovered his charade. Suddenly, a man in a black eye mask leapt out from behind a rock. He was dressed in the stars and stripes of the Colonial flag: red waistcoat, white ruffles, blue jacket. With a cutlass in his belt and a long rifle slung over his shoulder, he strode into the middle of the road with a flintlock pistol drawn in his black-gloved hand. "Your money or your life!" he shouted. Johnny stared down the thief.

"I already gave."

The thief was taken aback. "I don't think you heard me. This is not a polite request."

"Oh, I beg your pardon. You look like the other fellow I killed yesterday."

The robber laughed. "You have spirit, lad. I'll give you that. Such a clever tongue for a man with a gun pointed at his mouth."

"Are you in a play wearing a costume like that?" asked Johnny. "Those are gaudy colors for a man trying to ambush travelers."

"It strikes fear into my victims' hearts," the thief explained. "Everyone knows Samuel Culper, highwayman.'"

"Who?"

"Come now! You must've heard of me. I've pillaged and plundered my way from Braddock's Road to the Mohawk Trail!"

"Sorry, can't say I have. But I'd wager you know me."

"Your name, then. Let's have it."

"Johnny Whitman."

"The Dragonslayer?"

Johnny nodded.

"You drowned that Roanoke red at Godly Wood?"

"I did."

"I thought you'd be older. And taller."

"But I am better looking."

Culper laughed. "Well, this will indeed be an honor and a privilege to kill you."

"I thought you were a robber not a murderer," Johnny protested.

"That may be. But if I kill the Dragonslayer then I'll be known forevermore as the Man who Slew the Dragonslayer."

He fired his pistol. The lead ball stopped when it hit Johnny's dragon-hide coat. Stunned, his chest aching, Johnny swung his walking stick and cracked Culper over the head. As he fell to the ground, Johnny quickly relived the highwayman of his cutlass and rifle. Culper groggily sat up.

"Walk away now or I put you under the ground," Johnny warned.

"Alright lad," Culper chuckled, rubbing his head. "Seems I underestimated you. Tell you what, come with me. I'm on my way to a job that may suit you."

"You just shot me."

"It'll be worth the reward."

Johnny frowned. "I'm listening."

"The mayor of Alleghain has issued a reward for the safe return of his daughter who has been kidnapped by a dragon. The mayor is offering half his estate and his daughter's hand in marriage to any man who can rescue her. Naturally, every adventurous, able-bodied young man answered the call. All of them failed."

"And you want me to handle the dragon for you so you can get the girl?"

Culper shook his head. "I already have the secret that will be the creature's undoing." He held up a small, birch bark scroll.

"What is it?" asked Johnny.

"I got it from an Iroquois medicine man," said Culper. "They call it *orenda.* Inside are magic herbs and chert and incantations that will kill the beast when eaten."

"How do you know it will work?"

"One of the ingredients is from a dead dragon," said Culper. "I watched him cut out its heart and boil it in a pot."

"And what's to stop me from burying you in the woods and taking this potion for myself?"

"Because there's one final ingredient needed to make the spell work," Culper explained. "Only I know what it is."

Johnny thought it over. The shadows in the pines were growing longer around them. Soon it would be nightfall and the nearest shelter was still miles away.

"Let me live," said Culper. "Help me kill this monster and together we'll make our fortunes."

Alleghain, Connecticut was a clump of thatched-roof cottages nestled in the foothills of the Naugatuck Valley. What began as a homestead for Quaker missionaries who traded bibles and quilts to the natives in exchange for squash and maize had since turned into a bustling boomtown once the sawmill and logging industry took hold. Local woodcutters and fishermen said the dragon, "Bellowing Benedict", was named after Benedict Arnold, the war's most famous turncoat. The more superstitious among them believed this dragon *was* the old traitor come back to avenge his death by stealing young women from his birthplace. Known as an "Appalachian mountain-burrower" they said this variety didn't breathe fire and couldn't fly but its claws could crush a boulder and its thunderous roar caused avalanches. It lived in a cave somewhere near the peak. Johnny suggested they stop to buy supplies at the dry goods.

Culper cautioned against it. "I'm a wanted man," he reminded him. "Sam Culper isn't my real name, you know. They'll be more welcoming if we have the dragon's head and the mayor's daughter." Climbing up the steep ravines and gullies, past mossy trees and jagged rocks, Culper chatted. "Ever seen a hodag?"

"Can't say I have," Johnny panted.

"Ugly bastards. Like an overgrown crocodile with the face of a man. Or that thing in the Jersey Pine Barrens? Strange how there's so much variety here. In the old days, back in Wales or

France or Germany if you saw a dragon you knew what you were looking at. Oh, they may have called them wyverns, amphiptere or guivre, but they were all essentially the same. American dragons come in all shapes and sizes. Piasas, snallygasters, hoop snakes, goat-suckers down south. Curiosities so vile, no just or rational Creator could have made them."

After they had gone a little higher he added, "I read that Thomas Paine claims we live in an Age of Reason. What do you think?"

"I don't know what that means," Johnny confessed.

"It means now that man has subdued the earth, a day will come when we're no longer ruled by fear. Fear of nature. Fear of God. Fear of each other. That we possess the knowledge and virtue to better ourselves."

"This the opinion of a thief?" noted Johnny. Culper shrugged. After several grueling hours upward they reached a rocky barrow that led deep into the mountain. No birds sang in the trees. They'd seen no animals of any kind during their climb. Johnny went first down the dragon's tunnel. Keeping his palm against the clammy wall he descended into darkness. The sound of trickling water surrounded them as they moved further underground. They came into an enormous, pitch black cavern. Stalactites of pale, green phosphorous hung from above that offered the only luminance. Sitting in the middle of the cave was a young woman wearing a dress covered in dirt with tresses of long, thick, brown hair flowing all the way to the floor.

"Hello?" Johnny ventured. "Are you alright?" The girl didn't answer as if she hadn't heard him. She stared straight ahead. Her eyes wide but vacant.

"Look what she's sitting on," gasped Culper. Johnny saw between the girl's legs what appeared to be a large, purple-turquoise stone. As he looked closer he saw it had the same rough, shimmery surface as an abalone shell. Then he understood. The warmth of this den. The girl cradling it under her. It was a huge egg.

"She is my nursemaid," came an echoing voice behind them. They spun around to a grotesque sight. It resembled a gigantic salamander as tall as the cave ceiling, almost twelve feet high; easily forty feet long. Its body was made of gray, armored coils like an armadillo. Its mouth split into three rows of teeth with a pair of bent tusks jutting out the sides. Immense, pronged antlers grew from its head. Its lower haunches were covered in nine-inch porcupine quills.

"I don't want to eat you," said the dragon. "But I will if you go near her."

Culper notched a bolt in his crossbow with the magic herbs tied to its shaft.

"I can sense your intentions," the dragon warned. "The desperation in the air. You mean to take the girl from me."

Johnny motioned for Culper to stay his hand.

"Why do you keep her here?" asked Johnny, stalling for time. He realized the dragon was old and blind.

"I told you," the dragon replied. "She is tending the nest until my child is born."

"Is she here of her own accord?"

"I called to her and she came," said the dragon.

"She accepted a polite invitation?" scoffed Culper. The dragon bristled its needles. "I heard her wandering in the hills, picking elderberries," it murmured. "I looked in her eyes and guided her here."

"Hypnosis?" Culper exclaimed. "I'd heard it was possible."

"Ever since my mate perished some time ago I've been without companionship."

"How did your mate die?" questioned Johnny.

"I ate her."

"I've heard enough!" shouted Culper. "You devour one of your own then you ensnare this girl against her will?"

The dragon opened its mouth, either to roar or to object when Culper shot the arrow down the beast's throat. Whatever powder the medicine man had given him seemed to have the opposite effect. The dragon gnashed its triple set of teeth and shook so hard the cave walls around them began to rumble and crack as Culper wound another bolt onto his string. The dragon's eyes shone out of the green shadows. Culper was drawn into its dead eyes. Slowly he lifted his crossbow to his own chin. Pulled the lever. The bolt impaled his skull. Johnny ducked behind the girl. He drew Culper's cutlass, the blade poised above the egg. Keeping his eyes closed he shouted, "Another step and I break your hatchling in two!"

The dragon let out a deafening roar. The earth trembled. Green stalactites crumbled and fell. As the dust settled, the cave grew silent. After a long stillness a small voice pleaded, "Please, don't harm my child."

Johnny looked down. It was the girl who'd spoken. Yet the emptiness in her expression told him those were the dragon's words, not her own.

"If you have something to say," threatened Johnny, "Say it yourself, Benedict!"

After another, longer pause, the dragon spoke. "Benedict? Ah, yes. That's what they call me. After that Englishman in the funny wig. Although my name used to be 'Lyndworm.' A sailor with horns on his helmet named me this. It was he who took my sight. I let him live when he agreed to sail away and tell no one of this land. He's long since dead now. His children and his children's children, all gone and forgotten. Before that, the natives called me 'Warty Flint.' But I had another name before all these. My true name. It's been thousands of years since I've heard it. I can't remember. You see, before you Two-Legs came into being, the world was cold and dark and covered in ice. My people lived together then. In the clouds. On the crystal mountains. In the frozen oceans. In those days we were made of living fire, pure spirit. We melted the world with the heat of our ecstasy. The divine flame, Chaos. We burned brighter than the sun. And a new world, a green one, grew in its place. As the earth warmed we took on flesh. Forms similar to what you see now. In the beginning we had no need of speech. We had our dreams and songs. Not until the First Two-Legs came to our land, hunting us with their spears and arrows, did we learn their tongues. Your kind worshiped us once. When you wore no clothes, prayed to fire and spoke with trees. Until this was not enough. You were not content with fear and awe. You wanted our power for yourself. To hang us in your tents and wear us on your bodies. Your tribes banded together and turned against our kind. It was a betrayal. We were mighty, but few. Once we had our first taste of man we grew more reclusive and animalistic. Ruled by base desires. Less of us were born each generation as more of us were slaughtered. By the time white men arrived with their guns and cannons we had forgotten our songs, our souls."

The dragon stood in the dark, purring deep in its chest. Its antlers scraping at the rock ceiling. "Do you want to know a secret, little Two-Leg? The earth has no end, as most of your scholars fear. The truth is far worse. This world will go on and on and on. Oh, there will be an end to plants, to oceans, to animals. An end to man, to be sure. But the world itself shall outlast eternity. And we dragons with it. I have stared into endlessness. I have lived thousands of years in solitude and will live thousands more until Grandmother Moon ceases to rise. And in this world, without sound, without light, I will go on alone."

Johnny didn't know what to think. He almost felt sorry for this creature.

"You've come to kill me?" asked the dragon.

"Yes," said Johnny. "And return the girl to her family."

"That is impossible," the dragon sighed. "For I cannot die by a mortal's hand. And if you take the girl I shall be alone once more."

For the first time, Johnny considered the possibility he might never leave this cave. "You can't seriously think this girl will make your egg hatch?" Johnny reasoned. "Her warmth could never equal that of your mate. The egg has grown cold. You must know your child will never be born."

A guttural, raking noise shook the dragon. Johnny wondered if it was crying.

"It's true," said the dragon. "I have foreseen it. But I could not bear to give up." The dragon crawled further into the light, its quills prickling.

"Kill me," it intoned. "Please."

Johnny was at a loss for words.

"I don't want to wander the ages only to become the last of my kind."

"I thought you said…"

"No mortal weapon," rasped the dragon. "However, in that corner are my skins I've shed. Among them are the bones of my mate."

Cautiously, Johnny made his way to the opposite end of the cave where a bleached dragon skull rested on the stones.

"Take one of her claws," the dragon instructed. "Bring it here and pierce my side. It alone will be strong enough."

Johnny picked up a sharp bone that was curved as a scythe and almost as long. "Why did you kill her?" he found himself ask. The dragon let out a gravely breath.

"Our forbearers required food only once every century or so. Now we must eat almost constantly to keep our wits. We attacked each other in a fit of gluttony. To my eternal shame." The dragon stooped down, resting its chin on the hard, cold ground as Johnny carried the claw. "Here," the dragon motioned. "My neck is soft enough."

As Johnny raised the spike, his mind swam with questions. What other figures throughout its long history had this creature encountered? Alexander the Great, perhaps? Didn't he kill a dragon in India? Or was that Daniel in Babylon? If dragon's blood was so acidic why had he heard an old wives' tale that bathing in it could extend one's life? Wasn't there another story about a king who lived under the earth who abducted a girl to be his queen? If man was created on the Sixth Day did that mean dragons had been here a week before? Or even longer? And was it heroic for him to slay this blind, lonely wretch, too old and miserable to fight, resigned to while away its immortality in a gloomy hole? All these answers and more were about to die here.

"Promise me one thing…" the dragon murmured. Johnny inclined his head to listen.

The mayor's daughter returned to Alleghain, exhausted, dazed, as though woken from a dream, not knowing how she'd gotten up the mountain. She said she remembered a boy with a sword in a cave but not why she'd been captive there. The townsfolk knew it must have been Johnny Whitman the Dragonslayer who freed her. Although if that were the case, why had he not accompanied her to claim his reward? Days passed with no sign of the brave little farm boy. Legends of him continued to spread over the years. Everyone knew he'd gone out west with Lewis and Clark, fighting wendigos, paving the way for settlers. Others said, in his old age, he went north to hunt furry trout and jackalope with Fabian "Saginaw Joe" Fournier. Or south into Mexico to look for Aztec gold guarded by feathered snakes. Whatever became of him, the people of Alleghain were never troubled by dragons ever again.

Denmark Laine is a St. Louis freelance writer, poet and music critic whose work has been featured on Fox 2 KTVI, Subprimal Poetry, STL TV Live, the St. Louis Poetry Slam, *Eleven Magazine, Bad Jacket, Spartan Press* and *Book of Matches.* He is the author of *Exile On Cherokee Street*, *The Gods of Autumn*, *Thorazine Ice Cream Parlor* and *Smalltown Kings*. He wrote *The Absinthe Fountain* during the months of quarantine after reading a lot of William Blake and G. K. Chesterton's *The Man Who Was Thursday*.

www.ingramcontent.com/pod-product-compliance
Lightning Source LLC
Chambersburg PA
CBHW021739190726
48288CB00009B/3109